BAD DOGS

BAD DOGS

A BLACK CADET IN DIXIE

KEN GORDON

Charleston, SC
www.PalmettoPublishing.com

Bad Dogs

First Edition

Paperback ISBN: 978-1-64990-801-8
eBook ISBN: 978-1-64990-588-8

This book is dedicated to Terry Adams and Marlin Pryor—may your spirits find the rest you so desperately searched for here on earth—and to all the cadets who are, or were, in Dixie, but Dixie is not, nor was it ever, in you.

CHAPTER 1

I t was 6:45 pm, and as usual Jon Quest had not left the office.
He was the President and CEO of a large, diversified media
and consumer goods company, which owned television, radio
and cable stations, and several daily newspapers. In addition,
Jon's company produced movies, short films, and television sitcoms, owned several restaurants, and manufactured its own line
of packaged foods.

Though his job kept him busy, Jon also remained involved in
the community, his church, and more importantly, the lives of
his children and wife.

Jon rubbed the bridge of his nose as he leaned back in his
oversized high-back Italian leather executive chair. He had been
poring over the financials of a potential corporate acquisition
involving several radio stations in the mid-west.

Oblivious to the time, Jon voice-dialed Vivian Morgan, the
M&A vice president working on the deal and the one who sub-
mitted the financials to Jon.

"Hey, Vivian, I am reviewing the financials on this deal and
something is not making sense to me. I want to sit down with
you and the rest of the team later this week and go over it, line
by line, if necessary, until it clicks for me. This is a great opportunity, but I don't want to get over our skis on this one."

As Jon spoke, he was looking out of his seventh-floor window. The sky was a beautiful shade of amber and was littered with bleached, wispy clouds. The sun was lazily melting over the horizon, signaling the onset of yet another chilly fall night.

How romantic, he thought, completely zoning out on Vivian's ongoing commentary.

Jon's phone beeped, signaling an incoming call. Jon looked down at the caller ID on the phone console, which was sitting on his desk.

Jon gasped as the name "Lexie" appeared on his display.

"Hey, Vivian, hang on a second, I have another call coming in that I have to answer."

"No problem," remarked Vivian.

"Hello, my beautiful angel," said Jon with a big grin.

"Jon Quest, why are you still at the office? You know tonight is our night to host the family dinner! I was expecting you home early. I reminded you this morning."

"Oh my God, Lexie! I totally forgot! Okay, I'm leaving right now! I'll be home in 15 minutes!"

"Yeah, okay!"

"I will, baby! I'm on my way!"

Jon clicked back over to Vivian.

"Vivian, I have to go. I am late for my monthly family dinner, which I am hosting tonight! Call Deborah in the morning and have her put you on my schedule for later this week."

Jon swirled around in his chair and noticed Jessica standing in his office doorway. Jessica was the night cleaning lady and was used to seeing Jon in the office after hours. She would often come by between 6:30 and 6:45 pm to signal Jon that he'd better either call his wife or pack it up and go home.

Jon was grateful Lexie called him, even if she was not exactly ecstatic to find him still in the office.

One day a month, the entire Quest family broke bread together. Each month they alternated homes where they gathered. This month, the family was coming to his home, and his wife, Lexie, had already warned him not to be late. The tradition was started by Jon's mother because everyone was so busy with their careers and businesses, and "we may rarely see each other and take time to sit together". Though they regularly saw each other on Sundays at church, they were not always able to spend quality time, catching up on each other's lives, after the services were over. Jon's mother often lamented that living next to one another was not a substitute for being a family. "Being a family," she often said, "meant spending quality time together, knowing each other, and knowing what is going on in each other's lives".

He glanced at the clock on his desk, wincing as he realized the lateness of the hour.

Oh boy, he thought, *I am in trouble.*

Jon looked at Jessica and mouthed the words "good night." She smiled and nodded knowingly as she went on her way.

Jon placed the phone receiver into the cradle and watched as it automatically retreated into the top of his black marble desk. He stood up, stretched, and began clearing his desk. He placed his date book and several stacks of papers into his black alligator Lederer de Paris attaché case and snapped it shut. Jon scanned his desktop and deemed it once again neat and tidy. He hurried across his office and removed his jacket from the closet and slipped it on.

As he walked back to retrieve his attaché case, he scanned his entire office to ensure everything was in its place. Neatness was not only something he enjoyed, but he also needed the sense of calm and control it provided.

Jon loved his office. His large corner office was tastefully decorated and had the most spectacular view of both the city and the shoreline.

Jon personally supervised the layout, design, and decoration of his office. He wanted to ensure his office had a positive energy and spirit while speaking directly to Jon's unique personality. Though he was not one to micromanage, in this case, it was necessary and as a result, he really loved the look and feel of his office!

The decor was contemporary and masculine. The furniture was black with gold accents, the walls were tastefully covered with limited-edition African-American art, and the accessories were handpicked based on specific interests and matters of import to Jon.

Aside from his bedroom and enclosed back deck at his home, Jon's office was one of his favorite places.

Jon picked up his attaché case and walked toward the frosted-glass French doors, stopped, turned around, and made a final visual inspection of his office. It was a habit he had picked up from his time in the military. Everything had to be in its proper place.

As Jon rushed down the hallway, he thought about how much he loved his job and his company. Jon could find many reasons to be away from home 24/7, if his wife would permit it. A smile crossed his face as he thought of Lexie's reaction should he even think about not spending quality time with her and the kids. Remembering just how late he was, he passed up the elevator and opted for the stairs.

I hope Lexie's not too mad, he thought.

As Jon hurried through the lobby, he paused long enough to yell goodbye to Mark, the security officer seated at the large half-moon-shaped security desk, which was in the middle of the entrance lobby.

"Hey, Mark, I'm out of here!"

Mark gave him a thumbs-up.

"In trouble again, aren't you Mr. Quest?" Mark said jokingly.

"Yeah, but what would Lexie ever do if I acted right? But I guess I don't need to push my luck, huh? See you tomorrow."

"Yes, sir. Same time tomorrow?"

"Let's hope not!"

Jon hurried through the doors and looked down at his watch as he headed toward his car.

As the CEO, one of his many executive privileges included reserved parking. Jon had a reserved spot right in the front, which was a perk Jon could truly appreciate on a night like tonight.

Jon reached for the door handle and heard the doors unlock. He opened the door of his brown and bronze Audi R8, tossed his attaché case and jacket onto the passenger seat, and slid into its driver's seat. He pressed the button on the console and smiled as it rumbled to life. He adjusted the volume of his music until it played loudly enough for the people in the next zip code to hear.

Jon sped out of the parking lot and turned onto the street, heading for the freeway. As Jon turned onto the freeway, he thought about calling Lexie to confirm his ETA, but then he thought better of the idea. He was already late; no use getting fussed at twice.

Jon, conscious he was late, pressed harder on the accelerator, though he was already exceeding the speed limit. Driving in the far-left lane on the expressway, he tried to make up for working late. Fifteen minutes later, he exited the expressway and barely slowed as he made a hard right.

Corners like she's on rails, he thought.

A few minutes later, Jon was sitting at the entrance of Quest Estates, which featured a huge set of wrought-iron automatic gates with the letters "Q" and "E" on the left and right gates, respectively.

Quest Estates was several hundred acres and included four mansions, one guest house, one recreational facility, a private lake, horse stables, and a nine-hole golf course.

Jon reached over and pushed a button on his dashboard. The gates slid silently and slowly apart. Jon pressed hard on the accelerator and was thrown back into his seat as the R8 sped down the long main drive. He usually made a point of driving slowly when he entered Quest Estates so he could appreciate the landscaping and picturesque scenery. However, tonight, he just wanted to get home!

As he drove along, Jon noticed the herd of horses as they stood in the field grazing. Jon's horse, Lucky, was easy to spot as she was a honey-bronze color with a thick brown mane. Jon loved riding Lucky, though he was not able to ride as often as he wanted. Riding his horse was one of the few activities that really relaxed him and took his mind off work and problems. Jon also noticed Lexie's horse, Paso, grazing nearby in the field. They first saw Paso during a trip to Curacao, two years earlier. Lexie fell in love with the beautiful animal and purchased it during their trip.

After about half a mile, Jon approached the first mansion. It belonged to his youngest sister, Joyell. She was five years younger than Jon and quite a bit different. She was 5'6", dark-skinned, plus-size curvy, and full of energy. She loved to dance and enjoyed going out. She was married to a Marcus, a forensic psychiatrist, who was amiable and laid-back. Jon liked him and felt that he was good for Joyell. The couple had three daughters. Joyell was a criminal law professor at a local university. There was no doubt Joyell found her niche in that role. Joyell ambled through life until she happened upon juvenile criminal justice and was hooked. She graduated with a dual JD–MBA, then continued to secure a doctorate degree in juvenile criminal justice. She was a highly sought-after expert witness for many high-profile legal cases and had written a number of books on the topic. She had a way with seeing what others could not. She was often able to get "into the heads" of juveniles in a way that was determinative for treatment and case resolution.

Joyell drove a maroon Maserati Quattroporte, which she always parked in the middle of their circular drive. The fact that it was not there meant she was working late, like Jon, or at his house keeping everyone entertained, with her wonderful sense of humor, until her "Big Bro" arrived.

Up the road, about a half-mile or so, was the mansion of his older sister, Bernice. Bernice was eighteen months older than Jon. Bernice was 5'3", light-skinned, and a bit of a recluse. Unlike Joyell, she rarely went out, instead favoring an evening at home with family or at the JAM Center doing arts and crafts with her nieces and nephews. After studying theatre in Europe, earning a PhD in Critical Studies, then enjoying a number of years in front of the camera, Bernice now spent her time behind the camera producing, directing, and writing movies and television sitcoms. Bernice's husband, Angelo, a maxillofacial surgeon, was pleasant and gregarious. The two had four daughters.

Directly across from Bernice's mansion sat the recreation center. The three-story building housed a full basketball court, four racquetball courts, three tennis courts, an Olympic-size swimming pool, a large free weight and nautilus room, an aerobics and dance studio, a 1.5-mile jogging track, a movie theater, a video arcade, a game room with pool tables, a steam and sauna room, a five-lane bowling center, and a children's play area. Jon's children—two boys and two girls—would meet Bernice's and Joyell's children at the recreation center every evening after they finished homework to play games, shoot pool, or work out. The center was named the Josephine-Addie Memorial Center, after Jon's two grandmothers, and was referred to by the family as the JAM center.

At the end of the road, was the "Master Mansion", the residence of Jon's parents, Jon Sr., and Kathy. Jon Sr. and Kathy, business magnates, were enjoying the fruits of years of hard work in the fashion and home furnishings industries. When they were not jetting all over the world purchasing new clothing lines or inspecting their several manufacturing facilities, they spent their time on Quest Estates hanging out with their grandchildren.

Jon turned into his drive and proceeded to the rear of the house, where the five-car garage and guest parking spaces were located. As he came around the corner, he saw all his family's cars.

Uh-oh, he thought, *here we go*.

Jon pulled into the first available spot, turned off the engine, and quickly grabbed his attaché case, and jacket. As he collected his belongings, the side door opened, and Lexie stood quietly glaring at him.

No use in rushing now, Jon thought as he headed toward the door. Lexie met him before he made it halfway up the sidewalk.

"Hey, babe," Jon said as he leaned in to kiss his wife.

"Uh huh," said Lexie as she held up her hand and turned her face away. "You know I reminded you this morning! Really, Jon?"

"I know, honey, but—"

"Don't 'but, honey' me. This is just the same story, different day. Just hurry up and change. Everyone is in the study waiting on you!"

Jon rushed into the house and walked toward the study. He stopped long enough to say hello, apologize for being late, and promise to return from upstairs soon. Jon's two sisters, their husbands, and his mom and dad were in the study drinking coffee as they talked. As Jon exited and headed upstairs, Lexie entered the study. As she entered, he heard her apologizing to the others on his behalf.

What a woman! he thought.

He truly appreciated and loved his wife. They had been married twelve years and she was his best friend. There were so many things that had attracted Jon to her when they met. Not only was she stunningly attractive (FINE was the word he had often used), but she was also extremely intelligent, articulate, sassy, and a godly woman.

Lexie was just the kind of woman he had wanted and needed. Physically, she was extremely appealing. She was 5'5" with the most beautiful, smooth cocoa-toned skin. She was slender and curvy with bright eyes. She was gregarious, warm, caring, genuine, and never met strangers. She was a hugger and had a light that shone around her, drawing people to her like moths to a flame. Professionally, Lexie was an insurance executive and entrepreneur. Lexie was the CEO of an insurance company. In fact, she was the only female, Black CEO of a major insurance company. When they first met, Jon was immediately impressed with her sophistication, business acumen, and professional achievements. Aside from being the CEO of a major insurance company, Lexie also owned a string of water ice restaurants in several states, something she repeatedly shared with Jon was a dream of hers. Jon had no idea how she managed to do all she did, but her ability to do so was impressive. Spiritually she was one who allowed the light of Christ to shine through her as opposed to being one of those types that are hypocritical. Lexie was a woman who believed in prayer, in a relationship with Christ, and in allowing that relationship to make her a better, kinder, more empathetic person.

Lexie was perfect, to and for, Jon. It was as if when God made her He was thinking about Jon. She was everything Jon ever wanted, all the way down to her sorority! Jon especially treasured the alone time they spent together just talking. They often sat for hours on the screened-in deck talking about everything and nothing. Jon often wished every married couple experienced the same compatibility, satisfaction, and happiness.

Where was she twenty years ago? he thought as he rushed down the stairs. As Jon entered the study, Bernice was the first to turn to him.

"Well, it's about time!"

"Sorry, just one of those days."

"Oh, and I guess you're the only one who has those?"

Jon walked over to Lexie and kissed her on the forehead.

"Hey, Dad . . . Mom," Jon said as he crossed to his mother and kissed her on the cheek.

"What?" replied Kathy, having been engrossed in Joyell's latest humorous escapade.

Jon's mother was an amazing woman. She had built her company from the ground up and it had been a vision in her mind for over twenty-five years before it actually became a reality. She was a genius. She built a wildly successful company from the bottom up and still found time to raise a family and be a wife. She was a distinguished, sophisticated, and attractive woman. She was spunky, sassy, and energetic, but above all else, she was wise.

Jon's dad, a military veteran, was no-nonsense. He was often quiet, carefully picking when and where to speak. The man was as wise as an owl. Jon Sr. was notably just as much behind his only son as anyone. He, too, had been there for him through the years. Jon Sr. had truly shown Jon how the love of a father looked.

"So, Jon, are we eating tonight?" asked Joyell.

Jon glanced at his younger sister, smiled, then walked over and kissed her on the forehead.

"Excuse me, Mr. Quest? Would you care for coffee, sir?"

"Yes, as a matter of fact, I would," Jon said as Kati, one of their maids, handed him a coffee cup and saucer.

"Two lumps as usual, sir?"

"I'm so predictable!"

Jon sipped his coffee and looked around the study at the members of his family. He hated being late. He hated having everyone waiting on him.

"So, how was your day?" asked Kathy.

"I'm sorry, Mom, it has been a crazy day. As you know, we have the opportunity to purchase a radio station in—"

"Oh no, not more meetings and briefings!" interrupted Bernice. "Can we at least eat before we start with the briefings?"

Jon looked at Bernice with a scowl. She scowled back.

"Bernice, look—" began Jon, but was interrupted by the dinner bell.

"Dinner is served," announced Kati from the doorway of the study.

Everyone gathered themselves and moved toward the dining room. Jon placed his cup and saucer onto the end table and glanced at the mantle above. As he did, something caught his eye. It was not the myriad awards, plaques, citations, or certificates. It was something else. Something he had seen millions of times before. Something that had caused pain and pleasure, sadness and joy, fear and anticipation, and regret and reward. As he looked at his college degree, splendidly displayed on his awards wall, his eyes focused on the date. Twenty years ago today . . . Jon's flashed back to a place, long ago and far away. There, he heard yelling, screaming, running, shouting. . .

———————

"Brace!"

"You shithead! You better roll your shoulders back!"

"I hate you, toad!"

"You better rack your chin in!"

"Drop and give me fifteen!"

"Daddy! Daddy!"

Jon snapped back to the present as he felt someone tugging at his sleeve.

"Daddy."

Jon looked down at his five-year-old son, Kristian.

"Daddy, Mommy told me to come and get you. She said, 'don't let me have to come and get him myself.'"

"Okay, I'm coming right now."

"Daddy?"

"Yes?"

"Why are you always staring at that one big piece of paper on the wall?"

Jon looked down at his son, grabbed his hand, and headed toward the dining room.

"Well, son, I guess it's because of how difficult that one piece of paper was for me to get. A huge price came along with that piece of paper."

"So, what? I thought we were rich?"

Jon smiled at his son who was the spitting image of himself.

"No, son, your mother and I are rich. You and your brother and sisters are poor, unemployed, and broke. But I don't mean that kind of a price."

"Well what kind then?"

"Well, son . . ."

Jon's mind faded back to his freshman year at the Military University of The South.

CHAPTER 2

"**Q**uest! You better sing 'Dixie'!"

"Sir, no, Sir!"

"Quest, fall out to your left!"

"Boy, you better sing 'Dixie' now!"

"Drop and give me fifteen!"

"Sir, one, Sir. Sir, two, Sir. Sir, three, Sir . . ."

"Quest! You call those push-ups?!"

"Sir, yes, Sir!"

"Get up, toad!"

"Fall in!"

"Sir, yes, Sir!"

Jon had just finished up what was regrettably becoming part of his daily routine. Every day, upperclassmen would single Jon out, and other Blacks, to try and make them sing "Dixie" for their own amusement. Some did. Some did not. However, Jon never did.

"They'll see me in hell before I ever sing that song," Jon had once exclaimed to one of his buddies.

After completing the push-ups that were his punishment for refusing to sing "Dixie," Jon would then go to lunch or dinner and continue the remainder of his daily routine.

"Quest! You better brace!" Bracing was by far the most uncomfortable position Jon knew. It involved him clamping his arms so tightly to his sides that no one could see any light between the arms and the body. After that he would roll his shoulder blades completely back until they touched. Next, he would pull in his chin (or tuck it in, as they called it) as far as he could and stonily stare straight ahead. Often, upperclassmen would sneak up behind a freshman and devilishly try to pull their arms away from their body. If the toad was not braced properly, this made their arms swing up or back. It was this swinging that was usually the precursor to the toad dropping for push-ups or receiving a verbal lashing.

"Hurry up and prepare the table, you cumspots!"

"Quest, Military University of The South prayer . . . pop off!"

"Sir, I am a Military University man . . ."

"Shut up, boy! You ain't shit!"

"Pass the juice, Jonson!"

Mealtimes for Jon Quest, and in fact all freshmen, were an utter nightmare. Once the food was blessed, the four freshmen, called "Toads," were forced to cram preparing the table, pouring the drinks, reciting information upon request, and eating all into ten horrible minutes. There were even more challenges if a toad was disliked by any or all of the upperclassmen on his "mess." Jon Quest was one of those toads. Jon had been labeled a troublemaker early on in his freshman year. One reason for the label was the near fight he and another Black classmate had during the first week he reported to M.U.T.S. This near fight occurred when several of the Caucasian classmates obnoxiously began making some derogatory and insulting racial remarks about Blacks. Jon and Adam spoke up to let them know, in no uncertain terms, "not to go there!" They both voiced in no uncertain terms that they did not appreciate, nor would they tolerate, such remarks.

"Look, I don't play that shit," Jon had said.

"We ain't from down here in the South, and where we come from, if a mutha fucka says some ignorant shit like that, he gets his ass kicked. Trust me, you don't want to walk down the street, because one block will seem like a country mile," said Adam.

"Now we can get along for the rest of the year or we can go at it every chance we get together . . . it's up to you," Jon remarked.

"Hey, we're easy to get along with. I mean, me and Jon would be willing to ignore those previous stupid-ass remarks and chalk them up to ignorance, as long as they don't happen again."

Some of his classmates were offended. Others said the two were "overly sensitive." Still others just plain did not care. But regardless of who thought what on the matter, the parameters had been set, and they knew how these two "Black Yankees" felt.

"Quest, you got a joke for me, nigger?"

"Sir, no, Sir!"

"Quest, I thought I told you to have a joke for me today, or else!"

"Sir, no excuse, Sir!"

Every mealtime, the upperclassmen would make each toad tell a racial joke. Every mealtime, Jon would refuse. Therefore, after every meal, there Jon was doing push-ups until it was time to go to afternoon classes or study period.

"Murphy!"

Ben Murphy was one of the classmates that sat at the same table as Jon during mealtimes. Murphy, or Murph, as the upperclassmen called him, was from Augusta Georgia and was a "good ole boy" just like the other upperclassmen at Jon's table. Murphy played the French horn in the band and was in general a pretty likeable guy, except for today!

"Sir, yes, Sir!"

"You got a joke, boy?"

"Sir, yes, Sir. Sir what is the best kind of nigger, Sir?"

15

"I don't know, Murph," said the upperclassman, snickering. "I didn't know there were any good niggers."

"Sir, a dead one, Sir!"

The upperclassmen howled loudly with laughter. Jon sat there, clenching his teeth while hoping that the anger did not show on his face . . . too much.

"What do you think of that joke, Quest?" an upperclassman asked, laughing.

"Sir, no excuse, Sir."

This routine went on at every single meal, on every single day. Every few weeks, the toads would be shifted so they could sit at different tables. Sometimes Jon would go to a table with those that qualified as decent upperclassmen. Most of the time, however, there was at least one ignorant upperclassman at every table.

Jon had already gotten a reputation around his company. Everyone knew that Jon would not tell any racial jokes. It was this one fact that opened Jon up to constant harassment. At every table Jon sat, there was always someone who would demand he tell a racial joke. The horrible practice of telling racial jokes was disturbingly common at M.U.T.S. Unfortunately, Jon knew it would be open season on him because he refused to tell any racial jokes. Though he did not really mind the push-ups that followed every meal, the constant harassment he endured was a totally different story. This relentless harassment prevented him from eating. The lack of food and sheer hunger were what bothered Jon the most. Therefore, Jon decided he would have to do something. The unspeakable! The next time someone asked him to tell a racial joke, he would!

"Quest! You better swallow and pop off, nut!"

"Sir, yes, Sir!"

"Tell us a joke!"

"Sir, no excuse, Sir!"

"Quest, you better tell us a joke, you scum bucket!"

"Sir, yes, Sir!"

"Huh?"

"Sir, yes, Sir!"

"You're gonna tell us a joke?"

"Sir, yes, Sir!"

"A . . . uh . . . racial joke?"

"Sir, yes, Sir."

"Don't fuck with me, Quest! Are you gonna tell us a joke or not and it better be a good one?!"

"Sir, yes, Sir."

Jon Quest had been sitting at the table bracing. This very uncomfortable position, which was said to improve posture, made it doubly difficult to enjoy one's meal or eating as much as he could, as fast as he could, before the usual onslaught of harassment began. Now, Jon rushed to stuff his mouth with what he now knew would be the last food he would eat that day.

"Oh my god, Quest is gonna tell us a joke! Hey, Nick, c'mere, Quest is gonna tell us a joke."

Several upperclassmen huddled around the table in anticipation while seeming to revel in some sense of victory. Several of them wore the most ridiculous smug grins. Jon scanned the table with his eyes and noticed that all the White upperclassmen were eagerly awaiting his racial joke. They were confident, happy, gloating, even satisfied that they had finally broken Jon Quest.

"Awright, Quest, go ahead."

"Sir, yes, Sir," said Jon as he swallowed the last of his meal. "Sir, how do you save a drowning White man, Sir?"

The upperclassmen had looks that went from being noticeably puzzled to obviously irritated. They began glancing around at one another as if to say: "Hey, that's not a joke about a dumb Black, or stupid Pole, or a lazy Mexican."

"I don't know, Quest. How *do* you save a drowning White man?" snarled one of the upperclassmen.

"Sir, you don't know, Sir?"

"I said I don't fucking know, shithead!"

"Good," said Jon with a smile.

For a moment there was silence. No howls. No guffaws. Nothing, just pure and utter silence. It was like being in the eye of a hurricane. But remember, after the eye of a hurricane passes . . . you better hold on!

"Quest, you better brace!"

"You stupid nigger!"

"You got balls bigger than a bowling ball, but you're just as stupid as one too!"

"Quest, I want to see you in my room after mess," said the upperclassman who was in charge of the table where Jon sat.

"Quest, I'm gonna run your black ass outta here!"

Jon felt that he had just won a battle. He did not care what they did to him. He did not care how many push-ups he would have to do. It was all worth it. Yes, it was worth it this one time. One battle, however, does not win the war . . . but it can definitely do wonders for morale!

After that day, Jon was never asked to tell a joke at mess again. But once again, he confirmed the label "troublemaker" that he had already been branded with.

Aside from the racial jokes, there was of course the other reason for Jon's label. This reason was even bigger than the racial jokes. This reason was the one that created enemies not just in the corps, but also among the alumni and administration. That reason was Jon refusing to sing "Dixie," the unofficial fight song of M.U.T.S., and this put a huge target on his back.

"Quest, sing 'Dixie'!"

"Sir, no, Sir!"

"Quest, you better sing 'Dixie,' you little shit!"

"Sir, no, Sir!"

This exchange was also a part of his daily routine since the upperclassmen knew Jon would not sing "Dixie." Jon had sworn to himself and others that he would never ever sing "Dixie."

During Jon's freshman year, he met a family that lived in the local town where M.U.T.S. was located. The Simon family were active participants in the M.U.T.S.'s Cadet Adoption Program. The program paired freshmen that were not from the area with local families. This program gave the young cadets a local family to go to church with, spend weekends with, relax with, etc. The Simon family adopted Jon during his freshman year at M.U.T.S. This adoption proved to be one of the most significant and educational experiences of Jon's life.

Mr. Simon was a very large man, both in stature and intelligence. He stood about 6'6" and weighed about 320 lb. He had a full beard and mustache and always wore a smile. He was wise beyond his years. Jon never knew exactly how many years that was because he dared not ask Mr. Simon his age. Jon learned so many lessons from him, lessons that would ring true throughout the rest of Jon's life. Jon would savor those weekends when he could just sit and drink from Mr. Simon's deep well of knowledge.

Mrs. Simon, unlike her husband, was very petite and quiet. But boy could she cook! They lived about 12 minutes from M.U.T.S. in a cute little three-bedroom bungalow. The Simons had two children, a daughter, and a son. The son was older than Jon and Jon hardly ever saw him. The daughter on the other hand was a couple of years younger than Jon and proved to be very likable.

Jon was rarely able to relax unless he was at the Simons' house. During one particular visit, Jon relayed his daily "Dixie" routine to Mr. Simon.

"You have been refusing to sing 'Dixie'?"

"Of course," Jon replied proudly.

"And your refusal prompts punishment?"

"Yes, Sir. Push-ups mostly. But I can do push-ups until the cows come home!"

"Well why won't you sing 'Dixie'?"

"Why?!"

"Yes, why would you refuse to sing a song?"

"Because of what it is a reminder of and what it stands for!"

"Okay, what does it remind you of and what does it stand for?"

"It reminds me of oppression, ignorance, the ante-bellum South . . . It stands for racism, slavery, etc., you know, the old South! I for one don't wish I was in the 'land o' cotton'!"

"Hmmm," said Mr. Simon, thoughtfully. "Young man let me tell you something. You are a Black man. You are strong, independent, intelligent, resilient, feared, and talented . . . You cannot afford to be defeated by a song. Now every time you do not sing, they harass you more, correct?"

"Yes."

"Well, why don't you take their weapon and turn it on them?"

Jon studied Mr. Simon's face. For the life of him he could not figure out what Mr. Simon was asking him to do. Surely, he was not suggesting that he sing "Dixie."

"Let me explain . . ."

"Please do."

"Do you know who Uncle Tom was?"

"Sure, he was that shuffling, grinning fool that used to play up to the White folks."

"No, that's what they would like you to think. In truth, he was a Black slave who learned to get whatever he wanted by playing their game. He learned their game, became proficient, and eventually, better at it. Son, you can get whatever you want in life if you learn how to play the game. You do not get into the game voluntarily; you are born into it. That much you have no choice about. What you do have a choice about is how you play and how long you stay in the game. But remember, do not cry if they change the rules, or you are not successful your first time out. Too many of our young Black men are either out of the game, through death, or have 'gone straight to jail.' Son, neither of those outcomes are viable nor are they acceptable. If you don't learn anything else from me, learn that you must always play the game better than them. In order to play the game better, you must study your opponents, perfect yourself, use everything you learn to your advantage, and never, never let them know your weaknesses! In this game, you cannot accept defeat. There is far too much at risk! When confronted with a situation that would normally be a weakness, turn it around and make it a strength. You know the old saying: 'When life gives you lemons, make lemonade!' So, the next time they tell you to sing, do not let them defeat you. When they tell you to sing 'Dixie,' sing 'Dixie'!"

"Yeah, but how . . . I mean, I can't . . ."

"Wait a minute, son, hear me out. Do not sing the song, 'sang' that song! Sing it our way. The Black way."

"The Black way?"

"Yes, the Black way . . . with soul! Sing 'Dixie' like they have never heard it before. Get down with it. Make it Black! Give it rhythm. Give it soul. Sing it the best you can, until they can't stand it!"

Jon smiled.

"What a great idea," Jon whispered. "And I can definitely do it, too!"

Jon left the Simons' that day eagerly awaiting the next "invitation" he would receive to sing "Dixie." But before he would be ready, he had some preparation and practicing to do. He also had some people he wanted to prepare and practice with.

"Quest!"

"Sir, yes, Sir!"

"Sing, 'Dixie,' nut!"

"Sir, no excuse, Sir."

"Quest, you little piece of shit, you better sing 'Dixie'!"

"Sir, no, Sir!"

"Quest, fall out on the left!"

Jon Quest took a quick glance behind him. He then took one step back, did a left face, and ran quick-time to the left of the formation. At the left of the formation, he stopped, did a right face, took a couple steps forward, toed the line and stood there, bracing.

"Drop and give me fifteen!"

Jon instantly dropped to the "front lean and rest" position. He remained in this position, with his hat on his back and both eyes forward. He held his arms stiff and back straight while he waited for the command to begin. He stayed like this for what seemed to be 15 minutes.

"Begin!"

Jon pumped out fifteen push-ups and went back to the stationary "front lean and rest" position as he waited for the command to "recover."

"Recover and fall back in, shit for brains!"

Jon, with a smile on his face, returned to the formation and took a place on the front line.

"Sir, yes, sir! Fourth-year cadet Quest requests permission to sing 'Dixie'!"

Several upperclassmen turned around and stared at Jon in amazement. Word spread like wildfire and before Jon knew it, there was a crowd of upperclassmen standing in front of him. They were all abuzz about this miracle that was about to happen.

"Yeah, Quest, sing 'Dixie.' You'd better sing it loud and proud too, boy. We want the General to be able to hear it in his house!"

Jon, standing there in formation and bracing, took a deep breath. As he slowly let his breath slip out over his pursed lips, he relaxed his body and then shook his arms to loosen his body up even more. The upperclassmen looked on in bewilderment but said nothing. Neither did Jon. For almost a full minute, there was silence as Jon moved around making gestures and feigning relaxation and voice-warming exercises.

"Enough of this shit, Quest, sing the goddamn song!" said one upperclassman, impatiently.

Jon looked at the upperclassmen and smiled. He then looked around at the rest of his freshman classmates, who were bracing and were as puzzled as the upperclassmen.

"B boys!" Jon yelled.

Suddenly, Adam started imitating a beat box. Three other Black freshmen in the formation, Jeff, Louis, and James, started clapping their hands and stomping their feet in rhythm. All five of them began swaying back and forth and humming.

"Ohhhhh, I don't wanna be in the land of cotton, old times there should be forgotten . . .," Jon began singing in a soulful melody.

As Jon sang, Adam continued imitating the beat box. The other three cadets echoed each line while moving to the music, much like the soul groups of the 1960s. The five Blacks were "jammin'" with Jon singing the lead. They had practiced the moves and were executing them flawlessly. The cadets knew they would pay for this Nat Turner/Temptations demonstration, but it would be well worth it!

At this point, the rest of their classmates had stopped bracing and were howling with laughter. The upperclassmen, on the other hand, were in shock, paralyzed with disbelief. However, it did not take much longer for them to begin to recover.

"Brace, you faggots!"

"Rack your toady little chins in!"

"Quest, you're gonna get it, you little coon!"

"You stupid fucking niggers, you have done it now!"

"That's the last straw!"

"Your asses are grass!"

"Don't go to sleep at night!"

"You all may as well call Mommy and try to get a bus ticket outta here, cuz if you don't, we're sending you home in a fucking box!"

The upperclassmen began surrounding the cadets and were yelling and screaming from all different sides. They were going crazy. It was like someone had thrown a raw steak in the middle of a pack of wolves. There were a few upperclassmen that thought the whole incident was funny. They stood to the side and laughed. Of course, it was no surprise that most of them were Black. Jon, and his four accomplices, were harassed for the next several weeks. However, neither Jon nor any of the others were asked to sing "Dixie" ever again. Another battle won!

CHAPTER 3

Life was tough at M.U.T.S., so Jon found it necessary to get off campus just to retain his sanity. It was during these trips off campus that Jon partied, networked, pledged a fraternity, and pursued romantic interests.

The freshmen at the military university had curfews that made life even more stressful. Fridays and Saturdays, all freshman had to be back in their barracks by ten thirty. Failure to comply with curfew rules resulted in a prescribed period of confinement to the campus and to one's room. Jon, who already felt restricted enough, was never late. Close! But never actually late.

Life off campus was a needed distraction that made dealing with the racism on campus a bit easier. However, there was one thing on campus that made life easier than anything else for Jon—intramural sports.

Intramurals at M.U.T.S. were taken very seriously. The intramural participation level at M.U.T.S. was mostly 100%. Though participation was not mandatory, everyone was "highly encouraged" to participate. It was a well-known fact that "highly encouraged" translated to "you didn't have a choice". If one did participate, they did so with the understanding that the competition was fierce, and everyone played for keeps. Jon had many battle scars to prove this fact. Jon's battle scars included a gash over his right eye, which required twelve stitches, a disfigured middle finger on his right hand, and countless bumps, bruises, and other minor scars.

Once Jon began participating in the intramurals for his company, the pressure began to lift for him. After he began leading his teams to victory in such sports as flag football, team handball, basketball, and softball, the upperclassmen began to ease up. Traditionally, Jon's company had been horrible in all intramural sports. Therefore, this current winning streak attracted much attention. Jon began getting used to this easier life. For Jon, there was one particular incident that affected him greatly, much more than any other in his freshman year. During the peak of his intramural popularity, Jon was confronted by one of the officers in his company.

"Quest!" yelled a faceless voice during an evening formation.

"Sir, yes, Sir!" Jon knew the voice. The voice belonged to Ken Thoene, one of the platoon leaders in his company.

"Quest, fall out to the left!"

Jon took one step back, executed a left face, and could feel his shoe rub against the freshman that was in formation behind him.

"Ugh!" murmured his classmate.

"Sorry," whispered Jon as he double-timed past.

Upon reaching the left of the formation, Jon stopped, did a right face, and braced as hard as he could.

"Drop and give me fifteen, Quest!"

In one quick movement, Jon dropped to the ground, placed his hat on his back, and instinctively began pumping out the push-ups.

"Sir, one, Sir. Sir, two, Sir . . . Sir, fourteen, Sir. Sir, fifteen, Sir. Sir, Fourth Year Cadet Quest requests permission to recover, Sir!"

"No, Quest. You just stay there in the front lean and rest until I get tired!"

Jon remained in the front "lean and rest" for what seemed like an hour. His arms ached and he began to sweat. However, he refused to allow himself to shake. Shaking was a sign of pain and weakness, and he was not weak! In pain, yes! Weak, hell no!

Ken Thoene bent down and came face to face with Jon. He stared into Jon's eyes with a look of intense and bitter hatred. Jon studied the face perched in front of him, a face that was disfigured by prejudice and bigotry.

"I hate you, nigger," he snarled. "Do you know why I hate you?"

"Sir, no excuse, Sir."

"I hate you because you think you're hot shit. I bet you were hot shit in your high school, weren't you boy?"

"Sir, no excuse, Sir."

"Where did you go to high school, boy?"

"Sir, I went to high school in Philly, er, I mean Philadelphia, Sir."

"Well, you ain't back in 'Philly' in high school now! You're at M.U.T.S. You're deep down south where we used to hang happy niggers like you. Here you ain't shit. Just because you led the intramural football team to the championship game, and won, you still ain't shit. Here you're just a fuckin' panty waste! All you coons can do is dribble, run, sing, and dance. That's nothing new. I mean if it weren't for entertaining everybody else, how else would you get out of the projects?"

Ken Thoene stood up and looked around. Several upperclassmen were looking on. Clearly, they were amused.

"Get up, shit for brains. Fall back in."

"Sir, yes, Sir."

Jon thankfully scrambled to his feet quickly. His arms throbbed with pain. He placed his hat back on his head and immediately returned to the formation.

"Quest," said Ken Thoene, "I want to see you in my room immediately after second rest."

"Sir, yes, Sir."

Oh, shit, thought Jon.

Second rest was the signal to all freshmen that the 10 minutes they were allotted to "enjoy" their meal was over and they needed to exit the mess hall, post haste! For Jon, this next second rest would be one he would never forget.

Jon squared the corner as he double-timed toward Ken Thoene's room. As Jon stopped at the door, he did a left face. Jon had no idea what awaited him and paused shortly to consider the many possibilities.

"You gonna stand there all night?" said a voice from inside the room.

Jon quickly stepped up to the screen door, banged it twice, and stepped back.

"Sir, Mr. Thoene, Sir, Fourth Year Cadet Quest reporting as ordered, Sir!"

There was silence. Jon tried to focus his eyes to see anyone in the room, but it was much too dark for him to see. Jon waited a few seconds before he repeated himself.

"Sir, Mr. Thoene, Sir, Fourth Year Cadet Quest reporting as ordered, Sir!"

"Get in here, maggot!"

Jon ran to the screen door, opened it, and quickly ran into the room. Once inside the room, Jon searched in the dark for the full press. Upon locating the press, he ran over and placed the back of his heels along the bottom lip and stood there bracing as hard as he could.

There was silence again. The only sounds Jon could hear were the radiator hissing and a slight low murmur from the television. The room, which smelled of cigarette smoke, was hot, musty, and dark. The cigarette odor in the room was pungent and suggested that someone in the room was a heavy smoker. Jon stared straight ahead, but he was aware that there was someone other than him and Ken in the room. He could hear their breathing.

Jon stood motionless for what seemed like an eternity. He began to sweat and grow more and more afraid.

Why don't they say something? Yell at me. Call me a cumspot. Anything. Just say something! Please! thought Jon.

After what seemed like five hours, Ken Thoene finally spoke.

"You scared, boy?"

"Sir, no excuse, Sir."

No excuse was the safest answer. It was the answer you gave when you did not know whether it would be safe to say yes or no. It was like "pleading the 5th."

"You should be."

Suddenly, Jon felt a punch to his stomach. He fell backward into the full press. He lay on the floor, surprised, startled, scared, and holding his stomach.

"Get up, Quest!"

Jon scrambled to his feet, holding his stomach.

"Brace, boy! I thought you were a big-time athlete. Can't even take a little punch. Pussy! I don't like you. Did you know that Quest?"

"Sir, yes, Sir."

"Do you know why I don't like you?"

"Sir, no excuse, Sir."

"I don't like you because you are a dirty, smelly, stinkin', stupid nigger who shouldn't be in my school!"

Someone had turned the television off and now the room was completely dark.

"Hey! Why'd you turn off the television? I'm sure Quest wants to watch that new nigger show. What's the name of that show with the nigger doctor and his nigger lawyer wife?"

"The Bill Cosby show."

"Yeah, that's it! Ha! My grandfather would roll over in his grave if he were alive to see that shit!"

"Yeah, mine too. A doctor married to a lawyer and they are both niggers! That is so unrealistic!"

"Yeah, it just came out and I heard all the little niggers gather around their little black and white televisions to watch it."

"Quest, your people are so pathetic!"

"You want to know our message, Quest?"

"Sir, no ex. . ."

"Shut up nigger! Turn it up so he can hear real music!"

One of the faceless, nameless cadets in the dark, smoky, muggy room turned up the stereo. The song "We're Not gonna Take It" started blasting through the speakers.

Jon, who still felt a dull ache in his stomach, tried to see where Ken Thoene was, but couldn't. He heard his voice on his left but could not see him. Additionally, he heard another voice, an unfamiliar voice to his right.

"You know what we are gonna do to you, you little porch monkey? We are gonna rock you like a hurricane!"

At that moment, one of the cadets pressed a button on the stereo and a song by that same name started blasting.

"You ain't shit, Quest. We're gonna run you out of this school. You don't deserve to be here!" said another unfamiliar voice.

"Quest, why don't you just leave? Just pack up your bags, tell the school you would rather go back up North to an 'easier' school. Or tell them you need to be around your kind. Or better yet just quit and go back home to mommy!" said Thoene.

"Yeah, just transfer to one of those cheap nigger colleges," said a voice which sounded like Thoene's roommate.

"You can be free. No curfew, no uniforms, no push-ups. All the partying you can do. All the drugs and alcohol you can do. All the women you can screw! And we all know how much you niggers like screwing! All those fine Black women. Um, um, good. I wouldn't mind trying out one myself one day. I have heard how expressive they are in bed. Just think, a smorgasbord of black snatch. All you can eat! Oh, wait, I forgot, you Black boys don't eat that!" said the unfamiliar voice, laughing.

"Yeah, you can wear all those expensive jackets, shoes, jewelry, clothes. Or you can rob someone, take theirs, then shoot 'em. Isn't that what all you niggers do . . . kill each other over clothes, jackets, jewelry, shoes?" asked Thoene.

"Yeah, they kill each other over stupid shit like that. That's exactly what they do. They kill each other over colors and clothes. They talk about how many we killed down here in the South, but, shit, they kill more of their own over stupid shit than any of us ever did. If I didn't know any better, I would think the KKK was behind it!" said Thoene's roommate.

"Hey, that's fine with me. As far as I am concerned, they can keep on until they wipe themselves out completely. That's when we all will be better off. Shit just give them time," said the unfamiliar voice.

"Are you one of those, Quest? One of those niggers who'll kill your own kind over a pair of shoes, but can't stand up to one of us?"

Jon stared straight ahead. He refused to answer or acknowledge the question. He was angry but he was also very scared. As they talked to him, there was laughter throughout the room. Obviously, others had joined the little "party."

"C'mon, Quest! You can transfer and be around your own. You can have all the kitty kat you want, every night. You can have some white kitty kat and we won't even come string you up! Knowing how much you Black boys like our women, knowing you could have them ought to be enough to make you transfer!" said Thoene.

"Yeah, but you can only have white kitty kat if you leave here. You can't have it while you are here. Don't try what your roommate, or Terreaux, tried," said Thoene's roommate.

They were referring to Jon's roommate Paul, and Adam. Paul, who was White, was from the South. Yet, he only dated Black women. He had a huge boom box; he could dance and rap. A couple of times, people had entered their room and assumed Jon's desk was Paul's because of the boom box, rap tapes, and pictures of Black females that were housed there. Adam, on the other hand, was just a player who didn't discriminate.

"It's all pink inside!" he would always say.

Females from the opposite race had visited both Paul and Adam on campus. One day, however, they each received anonymous phone calls informing them that this was not a good or healthy practice as "the trees in the South were too tall and the ropes too short."

Shortly thereafter, Paul and Adam began to date within their own race with regularity. Not exclusively, mind you. However, they took great pains to see to it that their visitors were the same complexion as them.

"Wouldn't you like that, Quest? Wouldn't you like to be able to fuck every night? I know you could too. I have heard how you Black boys are in the bed. Real animals!" said the unfamiliar voice.

"Well, they're also animals outside of the bed, so that doesn't count," said Thoene.

"You're one of those pretty niggers, aren't you, Quest? One of those ones that all the women go for. You get a lot of snatch, don't you, Quest?" said the unfamiliar voice.

"Sir, no excuse, Sir."

"No excuse!? What are you, a faggot?" said the unfamiliar voice. "You must not like women, huh, Quest?" asked Thoene's roommate.

"Well, Quest?"

"Sir, yes, Sir. I mean, Sir, no, Sir. I mean . . . uh . . ." yelled Jon, confused.

Suddenly, someone's fist crash into Jon's jaw. As he fell down, someone struck him in the shoulder with a stick. On the ground, now, Jon curled up as his body was repeatedly rained upon with punches, kicks, and blows from sticks.

"Who the fuck do you think you are, nigger? You don't yell at me!"

"You think you're one bad nigger, huh?"

"You chicken-eatin' coon, I'll rip off your head and shit down your quivering esophagus!"

"Hey! Hey! Cool it, cool it," yelled Thoene's roommate.

As quickly as the blows started, they ended. Jon could hear heavy breathing. Some of it was from the inflictors of the beating, and some of it was his own. He lay there hurting, angry, and wanting to cry. He felt the blood dripping from his nose, lip, and above his eye.

I refuse to cry! I refuse to cry! I will not let them see me cry! As long as I am here, and no matter what they do to me, I will never let them see me cry! thought Jon.

"Get up, Quest," said Thoene. "Help him up!"

Jon staggered to his feet and groped for the full press. Once he found it, he positioned his heels against the bottom lip. Before he began bracing, he looked around the room to see who had been assaulting him. The faces he saw were disfigured with hate, just as Thoene's had been. He burned each of the faces into his mind. These were people he would never forget. One day each one of them would have to answer to Jon, that much he vowed!

Some of the faces were familiar. Several were not. There was Paul Rankin, Ken Thoene's roommate, a high-ranking senior officer. There was Randy Thomas, Bill Tolley, Jud Norment, and Al Bulowalski, all high-ranking seniors. After getting a good look at the men, Jon began bracing.

Jon's looking at them surprised them. He was not supposed to look at them. He was supposed to be so scared he dare not look around. The fact that he looked at all of them, and recognized some, bothered them. They were afraid. Jon could see it in their eyes. They knew Jon had them by the balls.

"Quest, I will not allow a nigger to stay in my company. I will not permit you to graduate. I'll kill you first!" snarled Ken Thoene.

"Quest, you get a good fuckin' look at us?" a voice asked.

"Sir, no excuse, Sir."

"Well, you better forget every face you saw, because if you breathe a word of this to anyone, we will be back. And if we have to come back, nothing and nobody in hell will keep us from finishing you off," continued the faceless voice.

"And, Quest, if we do come back for you, no one will be there to pull us off of you," said Ken Thoene.

"Now leave, Quest!"

"Sir, Mr. Thoene, Sir, Fourth—"

"Leave!"

Jon ran out of that room and all the way back to his room as fast as he could. Once inside his room, Jon exhaled and inhaled deeply as he tried to calm himself. He walked over to his mirror and stared at himself. Because he had curled himself up, he was not disfigured. However, there was an open cut above his eye and his lip was busted. As he stared at himself, Jon made himself and all the other Blacks coming behind him a promise:

"No matter what they do to me; no matter how they treat me; no matter how they beat me; they will NOT make me leave. I will learn their game and beat them at it! I will NEVER leave until I wear a Military University of The South band of gold and possess a piece of sheepskin with my name on it. That will prove

I am as good or better than any of them. I will sacrifice all I must in order to make this happen. They cannot touch me. I can do it! I MUST DO IT! Not just for me, but for all who are coming behind me. I am Black. I am strong. I am proud! I pledge this today on my own life!"

Though Jon heard his own words, deep down inside Jon wanted to call his mother. He wanted to talk to his dad. But he could not. Jon Sr. had drilled into Jon that men handle their problems. They do not run to mommy or daddy. They do not whine and complain. They make the bed, then they lay in it without grumbling or crying. Jon wanted to call his family because he knew they would tell him everything would be okay. He wanted to call Bernice because she would say out loud all the things Jon wished he could say. He wanted to call them and let them know what was going on. But Jon Sr.'s words stuck in his brain.

"Real men handle their own issues. Real men do not run. Real men do not cry. Real men do not call mommy"

Jon was fiercely independent, so it was often easy for him to just "go it alone". He never complained or talked to others about what was happening to him. He did not talk to his parents. He did not talk to his sisters. He did not talk to anyone. On the few occasions, he did, like the time with Mr. Simon, he felt stupid, weak, foolish.

No, he could not call his mother. He could not call his family. As close as they were, this was a man's problem and he had to handle it like a man. He had to handle it like Jon Sr. said. He wanted Jon Sr. to be proud of him and proud that he was a man.

Internalize the pain.

Turn the pain into fuel.

You made this bed. You made this decision. You made this choice. You must lie in the bed you made.

Jon climbed onto the top rack. He decided he must lie in the bed he made. At that moment, with a swollen eye, cuts on his face, bruises on his arms, ringing in his head, he would lie in the bed made for him earlier that day, but in this bed, on this night, he would cry. No one would have to know.

Jon then turned to the wall and began to cry.

CHAPTER 4

A t the dinner table, Jon was silent. He stared at the other end of the huge dining table. For a while, no one spoke. Finally, as was her straightforward way, Bernice was the one to break the silence.

"Yeah, I remember your freshman year. I was so afraid for you and there were many times I didn't know if you would make it. I wasn't even saved then, but I prayed for you."

"Oh?" said Lexie.

"Well, we are talking about the south," Bernice said. "You know where people don't always recognize that things like slavery and lynching are illegal. I was afraid they would either kill him or he'd kill one of them."

"Nah, I knew he wouldn't leave," said Joyell with a reassuring smile. "But I used to wonder if he'd make it through all four years without getting kicked out."

"I worried more about his health than anything else," said Kathy. "He didn't exactly make a habit of taking care of himself as well as he should have. I'm sure you know all about that by now, Lexie. I remember when we went down for the Family and Friends Weekend. Jon had only been there eight weeks and he had already lost 25 pounds. Jon had always been thin, but by then he was skinny as a rail!"

"She took one look at him and started crying," said Joyell.

"Yeah I remember when Mom called and told me about it. She sounded so hurt and worried. She said he was, well . . . different," said Bernice.

"You mean he wasn't hyper, gung-ho, laughing, joking, and talking a mile a minute," said Angelo, Bernice's husband.

"No, he was just the opposite. He was really quiet and acted really weird," said Kathy.

"He was constantly fidgety and looking around. He acted really nervous and restless. It was really quite painful to see."

"It was depressing to me," said Joyell. "He was nothing like the big brother I knew. He was skinny and looked like he hadn't slept in weeks. I was afraid for him. Looking the way he did, I figured he would have to be hospitalized soon thereafter."

"You are so dramatic!" Bernice said to Joyell. "I figured he would have to be hospitalized soon thereafter," she mimicked.

Joyell smiled wryly as she leaned over and whispered into Bernice's ear.

"You know, I hate it when you say that!" Bernice snapped.

"Say what?" inquired Kathy.

"Uh, nothing, Mom," said Joyell quickly.

"Anyway, I started sending him care packages. I was in college then myself, but I knew he needed it," said Bernice.

"There were many nights that Jon told me he wouldn't have made it without his family. That's why he is the way he is with regard to all of you. He doesn't play when it comes to his family," said Lexie.

Jon was not speaking. He shifted in his seat and cleared his throat. Everyone looked at him, expecting him to speak. The expression on his face never changed and he continued to remain silent. His body was sitting there, but Jon was obviously in his own world. In the room there lingered an envelope of silence.

Lexie, knowing that her husband was now miles and years away, spoke up.

"Let's all move to the study for coffee and dessert. Jon will join us shortly."

Individual conversations began as everyone slowly moved into the study. Everyone, that is, except Jon and Lexie. Moments later, the dining room was empty and just like before it was devoid of sound. Lexie sat motionless as she stared intently at her husband.

Lexie did not dare to try and bring Jon back to the present. She had seen him in this frame of mind many times before. Jon was there reliving the pain, the frustration, the confusion. Lexie knew and she understood. She reached out and took Jon's hand into hers. Lexie gently stroked his hand as she looked deeply into his brown eyes. As she looked, Lexie could not help but admire his perfect eyelashes and eyebrows.

I know women who would kill to have those, she thought.

Lexie truly appreciated her husband. When they first met, she knew immediately that he was everything she ever wanted. He was strong, funny, intelligent, professional, refined, and a man's man. She was immediately attracted to him, she remembered. He was a good, kind man. He was spiritually strong, emotionally intelligent, and psychologically healthy. Jon was all that she had asked God for after surviving her experiences with insecure, narcissistic children in grown men's bodies. Lexie truly thanked God for her husband daily.

Suddenly, Jon rose to his feet and looked around.

"Welcome back," Lexie said with a smile.

"Where is everyone?"

"In the study, having coffee and dessert."

"Why aren't you in there?"

"Because you are in here."

"Oh."

"Are you ready for some dessert?" Lexie asked as she stood up.

"Yeah, I am, but we have company now. I'll settle for a nibble," said Jon as he patted his wife on her behind and tried to kiss her neck.

"You are so fresh," Lexie said, moving away from Jon. "Be good. You know we have company!"

"Are you suggesting I am not always good?" asked Jon, playfully, as he embraced Lexie.

"Stop, I say," said Lexie while feigning resistance. "You are so bad!"

"I know and that's what you love about me," said Jon as he ran his tongue around the outline of Lexie's lips.

"I've wanted to kiss you all day."

"You haven't seen me all day," insisted Lexie!

"But I have still wanted to kiss you all day," said Jon, smoothly.

They looked deeply into each other's eyes as their faces moved closer to one another. Jon smelled the sweet fragrance of perfume as his wife's face neared his. He could almost feel the smooth, soft skin that graced her beautiful face. They both closed their eyes as their mouths opened and welcomed one another's tongues. Finally, Jon would enjoy the kiss he had been wanting and waiting for all day.

"Ah, um, ahem! Ahem! Grooooooooosssssssssss!!!"

Jon whirled around toward the doorway.

"Excuse me, love birds, but as soon as you two get done groping each other, you can join the rest of the family in your study," said Joyell, mocking impatience.

"We're on our way," said Lexie, straightening herself.

"Yeah, on your way to what? Certainly not the study," sang Joyell.

"We are a little busy right now," Jon said as he tried to wave his younger sister out of the room. "We will be there in just one minute."

"Oh, that's all it takes you, stud? Just one minute? A one-minute man? What?!" teased Joyell.

"We are on our way now," said Lexie, pulling Jon toward the door.

"Oh, awright," said Jon as he gave Joyell the hairy eyeball.

Lexie took Jon's hand and led him into the study. In the study, Jon smelled freshly brewed coffee and the cinnamon from Lexie's bread pudding.

"Ummm," said Jon, "is that bread pudding?"

"Yes, sir," said Kati. "Would you care for some, Mr. Quest?"

"Yes, Kati. Please bring him a bowl of bread pudding and a cup of coffee, with one lump. Also, bring me a small bowl and a cup of tea with two teaspoons of honey," said Lexie as she settled down into her chair.

"Yes, ma'am. Anything else?"

"No, that will be all, thank you."

"You know, it is absolutely amazing, I never knew very much about any of that stuff. I mean, no one ever talks about it. I knew Jon went to the Military University of The South, but I had no idea he had all of those problems there. I mean, I did, but I didn't. Is it something you're ashamed of, Jon?" said Marcus, Joyell's husband.

"No, it's not that I am ashamed. It is just that it was a painful part of my past, which, most days, I'd rather leave in my past."

"Then what made you talk about it today?" asked Angelo.

"It's probably the fact that today is the twentieth anniversary of his graduation, and when he looked at his degree when he first walked in, he couldn't help but remember," said Jon Sr.

Jon looked at his father and nodded in agreement. It never ceased to amaze him how wise his dad was.

"So, I take it life didn't get any easier," said Marcus.

"That's the understatement of the year," said Bernice.

"No, life didn't get any better. But as a matter of a fact, for the majority of my sophomore year, it didn't get any worse, either. Soon, I was elected as the president of the Black Student Society. At that point, the line was drawn. Many of the White cadets knew I was influential. Many of the administrators, teachers and staff knew I was influential, also. However, it wasn't until I was elected unanimously as an upcoming junior that their fears were confirmed. I mean, this was a first; it had never happened at the Military University. I was pretty low-key my sophomore year as I continued to learn to play their game. I was learning my way around their system. By the time my junior year rolled around, I was ready. I had my power base. I had my crew. I had the knowledge and I had acquired some clout. I had identified many areas which needed to be changed and was prepared to offer real solutions to implement those changes."

"Here you are, sir," said Kati, as she handed Jon his dessert and coffee.

"And ma'am . . . here is yours."

"Thank you, Kati," said Jon and Lexie almost simultaneously.

Jon took a sip of his coffee. "Ahhhh, good coffee! Almost as good as Waffle House coffee!"

"Ewwwww!" gasped Bernice. "Seriously?!"

"Oh, he is dead serious," remarked Lexie. "He loves Waffle House coffee!"

Jon put a large portion of bread pudding in his mouth. His eyes rolled up toward the ceiling as he chewed slowly and deliberately.

"Somebody please take off my shoes so I can wiggle my toes!"

"He is so famous!" remarked Lexie as she rolled her eyes.

"Gurl, I don't know how you put up with him! If I had to live with him, I think I'd commit suicide," said Bernice.

"Yeah, well, it would be suicide for Lexie to try to live without me!"

"You are absolutely right, dear. I don't know what I would do without you," Lexie said softly.

"You doggone skippy you don't," smiled Jon as he settled into his favorite leather chair.

A few bites later, Jon finished his bread pudding and sat the empty bowl on the end of the table, next to his chair. He leaned back, crossed his legs, and thoughtfully sipped his coffee.

CHAPTER 5

A s Jon sipped his coffee, his mind drifted to the beginning of his Junior year. Jon was elected as the Secretary of the Black Students Association his sophomore year. The President of the Black Students Association, a senior named Jace Mbali, was a mentor, role model and fraternity brother to Jon. From the time Jon was elected as secretary of the Black Students Association, Jace began preparing him to become the president. By the time Jon's junior rolled around, Jon was ready.

Jon returned for his junior year with big plans for the BSA. He wanted to move the organization from a social, party organization, that was not taken seriously by the administration or the other students on campus, to a bona fide service and social justice organization. However, in order to move the group in that direction, Jon would need help.

When Jon arrived on campus for his Junior year, the first thing he did as the newly elected president of BSA was call a meeting of the most influential Black cadets on campus. He gathered members of the various fraternities, key members of the various athletics teams, members of the religious clubs, and other Blacks who were influential in their sphere.

The group of Black cadets met one afternoon, during their first week back, in an empty classroom in the Mathematics Building.

"Man, I had a boring summer!"

"Oh yeah, why?"

"It was so long. I mean all I did was work. I had planned on going to summer school, but I didn't really have to . . . so I went home instead."

"I wish I would've been so lucky. I was on a cruise this summer. It was a trip. I mean it was fun and all, but damn I stayed tired!"

"I wonder what this year is gonna be like?"

"It's gonna be the shit. I mean we got our blazers and all!"

"The year ain't gonna be all that. I am done taking my electives. That means I'll be into my mandatory major courses. That will mean a lot more studying. I mean some of us are here for an education. I was tempted to take underwater basket weaving as my major like some of you, but as many of you know, I decided to take the easy way out and major in physics."

"We sho' is impress'd wi' dis big ole smart darkie we gots sit'n heaya in front 'us!"

"Fuck you!"

"Yas suh, boss. What evah you say!"

"Well, I for one can understand what he's saying. As a matter of a fact, I know several of us can. With my major courses coming up, football, choir, the literary society, and the Black Students Association, I'm barely gonna have time to get off campus to any frat meetings!"

"Don't you mean frat parties? That's really what you're worried about, ain't it?"

"Do you blame me?"

"Hell, naw. Not at all. I have the same concerns."

"Sounds to me like some of you fellas ain't gonna have time to even get with any lady's this year. That's how it sounds to me! All I got to say is that when you get horny, don't look at me. You better look at Rosy."

"Yeah, like one of us would really want yo' nasty, ashy, hairy ass!"

"Who is Rosy, anyway?"

"Yeah right, like you don't know!"

"I don't."

"Rosy palm and her five sisters!"

The cadets howled with laughter.

"Anyway, all of us have a lot on our plates. The question now becomes what all are we gonna be doing in each of the areas. We have to try to maximize our efforts. We all know what to expect this year from football."

"Yeah, especially after going to the play-offs last year. For which I think we all should give Tony a pat on the back when we see him this year in the BSA meetings."

"Yeah, well what about the choir? What are we gonna be doing in there this year?"

"Yeah, Derrick. When do we start practicing?"

"When is our first performance and where?"

"Well, we are scheduled to perform at Bishop R.A. Nelson's church in the third week of school. So, we will have to start practicing as soon as everybody comes back."

"Man, how in the world did you get us to be able to perform there?"

"Yeah, you know nobody just gets in that church."

"Man, I love to hear Bishop Nelson preach, though."

"I know, he's awesome!"

"I just wish his church were closer, instead of all the way up in the northern part of town. I know I would be there every chance I got if it were closer."

"Aw man, that's solid! I can't wait."

"Ay, Jon, when is our first BSA meeting?"

Everyone turned to Jon, who had been sitting quietly, deep in thought.

"Earth to Jon."

Jon looked around the room at the cadets. There they all sat staring at him, awaiting an answer.

"What?"

"Damn, mutha fucka, where were you!? We asked when the first BSA meeting is!"

Jon looked from face to face.

He looked at Adam Terreaux, his vice president. Adam was a stocky 5'10", with light-brown skin and wavy brownish-red hair. He had a masculine face with a strong jawbone. Adam, who was from Baltimore, had an ego twice as large as he was.

Jon looked at Tyrone Donald, his roommate and fraternity brother. Tyrone was 5'7", plump and always smiling. Along with his round head, his features earned him the nickname Buddha. Tyrone, who was from Washington, D.C., was a hustler by nature. Straight from the streets, he had an angle to everything. The thing Jon loved about Tyrone was that he was always thinking and never permitted himself, or his boys, to be put in a compromising position.

Then there was Derrick Avery, his choir director. Derrick, an offensive lineman on the football team, was an intimidating presence. He was, however, one of the most good-hearted people Jon had ever met . . . and boy could he sing! He was glad Derrick was in his corner!

There was Theo Poole, a senior in Jon's company. Theo, who was tall, lanky, and not at all intimidating, was a good-hearted person. Theo was one of those people that is just nice by nature, with no intent to do harm to anyone. Theo helped Jon a lot during his freshman year, and Jon was very loyal to him for it.

There was Tim Matthews, who was a muscular 6'1". Tim had a flashing smile full of bleached white teeth. You almost never saw Tim when he was not smiling or joking. He was a boxer who had a love affair with any kind of bread. He was affable and moved easily between all groups at the university.

What was interesting was putting Tim and Adam together, since Tim's ego was just as large as Adam's. Talk about two Alpha Dogs!

However, to take those two and then put them with Jon was really something! There would be so much testosterone in the room, it would make one dizzy! Many people said the reason Tim and Jon got along so well was that they were always so busy bragging on themselves, they did not get a chance to get on each other's nerves.

Jon looked at Evan Norton. Evan was both a fraternity brother to Jon and an officer in the BSA. He was a year under Jon and among the ones Jon helped during their freshman year. Evan, who was an impeccable dresser, was attending M.U.T.S. on a special naval scholarship. Under the provisions of this scholarship, Evan's college tuition, room and board, and books were paid for. In addition, he was given a stipend every month. *What a sweet deal*, thought Jon.

There were others in the room, including Joseph "JT" Thomas, who was the sergeant-at-arms for the BSA; Tommy Cline, a football player and one of Jon's personal bodyguards; McKenzie Summers, a frat brother and constant companion, friend, and confidante to Jon; Nate Wright, the secretary of the BSA; Albert Miller; Richard Payne; Antonio Byers; Kieran DeSaussure; Will Powell; Jerry Woods; Ellis Underhill; and others. All were waiting for Jon to answer their question.

"As you know, we normally meet the first Tuesday in September. That is after everyone has been back a couple of weeks and has had a chance to get their classes straightened out. I see no reason to change that."

"You know, Jon," began Albert, "I just knew you were going to get Regimental or Battalion staff I mean, damn! At worst, I figured you'd get company First Sergeant!"

"Yeah, me too," agreed JT. "You got screwed, cuz!"

"Yeah, but we all know the skinny on that shit," said Tyrone.

"They are scared of you, man," said Will. "I mean, don't fool yourself, they know how much juice you got. They know, and it scares 'em."

"Don't think they didn't hear about the election, either," said Antonio.

"Oh, you know they did," agreed Jerry.

"What about that article he wrote?" said Tommy.

"Yup, exactly. They know they dealin' with some bad mutha fuckas now!"

The "steppin' and fetchin'" days are gone, said Adam.

"Yeah, right! We may as well buckle in for another ride on the 'Mighty Whitey Express.' Ain't nuthin' changed in 150 years, and ain't nuthin' gonna change now," said Richard. "You know the deal . . . another year of the same old shit!"

"Naw, fuck that," said Jon, finally speaking and rising to his feet. "We ain't gonna be on that same mu'fuckin' roller coaster this year! This year is gonna be different. It's gonna be different because we are in charge and we ain't gonna let that shit slide. As a matter of a fact, I been thinkin' . . . I'm gonna meet with the regimental commander. I'm gonna let him know we are not gonna deal with the same old shit this year. We ain't gonna deal with the jokes, the snide comments, the off-color remarks, the harassment of our freshmen, none of that bullshit! He gonna hafta call all his company commanders together and address the issues of racial jokes, off-color remarks, and general racial harassment. Because we ain't havin' it! Theo, I want you to arrange a meeting between the RC, me, Adam, and you. And I want it done yesterday!"

"All right Jon. Any preference with regard to the day or time?"

"Nope. We'll meet him anywhere, at any time."

"All right, I'll let you know something in the morning."

"Good, thanks. Now as for the rest of you, I need you to put your ear to the ground and find out what racial things have happened so far this year. Any and everything. You know here at the M.U.T.S., there are no thin lines. When they do things, it is blatant. So, find out and get the specifics. Unless you have anything else, the meeting is adjourned."

Talking among themselves, the cadets began to filter out of the room. A few lingered behind to have a word with Jon. After 20 minutes, the only ones left in the room were Tyrone, McKenzie, Evan, and Jon.

"Well, this is gonna be a fucked-up year. I can feel it in my bones," said Jon.

"Whaddya mean?" asked Tyrone.

"I don't know. I can't explain. It's just that . . . You know, it seems like everything has been stewing and it is bound to blow, sooner or later."

"Well, for all of our sakes, I hope it is more later, than sooner," said Evan.

"Yeah, I know what you mean," said McKenzie. "I just want to enjoy my upper-class privileges and try to forget about the rest of this . . ."

"Speaking of that," interrupted Tyrone. "The AKAs are giving a 'Welcome Back To School Party' on Friday night at the City College Student Center."

"Yeah?" said Evan.

"We goin?" asked McKenzie.

"I don't know if I am," said Evan. "Cyndee will kill me if I don't spend some serious time with her this weekend. You know we have a lot of catchin' up to do."

"Man, you got the rest of the weekend to spend with her. You better take advantage of this night out with the boys. Plus, Cyndee doesn't even have to know you went out. Tell her you got in trouble and got some confinements," said Tyrone. "Man, it's too early in the year to be pussy whipped!"

"Well, I know I'll be there. I'm on the hunt. I need some new stuff. Call me a ho' if you want to, but I plan on having me some fun this year. No commitments, no ties, no relationships," said Jon.

"Yeah, we'll see. We've heard that story before," said McKenzie, with mild disgust. "No commitments, no ties, no relationships . . . Nigga, you'll be the first one in a relationship this year!"

"Hey, Tyrone," began Evan. "You been down there to check out the new crop, yet?"

"Yep, yep! They got some bad sistahs down there! I mean, that is in addition to what they already had!"

"So, the hunting should be good on Friday?"

"Oh, and you know this!"

"Well, if that's the case, I think I just slept through morning muster and got five confinements! McKenzie, how's Shelley?"

Shelley was McKenzie's girlfriend from last year.

"She's fine . . . I guess."

"You guess? Aw shit, trouble in paradise. Don't tell me you cut her loose. Or did she have the scissors?"

"What can I say? I'm a young, virile man. Now drop it, awright?"

"Yes, Sir," Evan said as he rose to his feet and executed a less-than-perfect hand salute.

As he sat down, he leaned over to Tyrone and whispered loudly to him. "She had the scissors!"

Jon, Tyrone, and Evan laughed. McKenzie disgustedly waved them all off.

"Hey, Mack, a word to the wise," Jon advised. "Just make sure if you are not completely done with Shelley . . ." He paused, looked around the room, and motioned with his index finger for

McKenzie to come closer. "Don't bring her around Tyrone. I mean you know how he is. It just don't feel right unless one of his boys has been in it!"

All four cadets exploded into laughter.

"Man, you guys better get back to the barracks," said Jon with tears in his eyes.

The cadets gathered their belongings and walked slowly out of the room, down the stairs, and out of the building. Once on the outside of the building, they paused momentarily for good-byes. Then each one headed for his respective room.

"Jon! Jon!"

Suddenly the door to Jon's room flew open. Evan stood, out of breath, in the doorway.

"Jon, you better come quick. The guys over at 'H' company are fucking with Clark."

"Wait a minute. Slow down," said Jon calmly as he laced up his spit-shined shoes. "What guys, what Clark, and fucking with him how?"

"Some upperclassmen over at 'H' company have our Toad Clark in their sally port and they are giving him hell. They won't let him go by to get to formation. They're saying he said something to one of their upperclassmen, now they won't let him pass. They're telling him to go the other way and some guys from 'G' company are telling him he can't come their way. Jon, they're really fucking with him good. Some of our other upperclassmen have tried to get him but they won't listen to them either."

Jon, who had been getting ready for evening formation, picked up his cover and his clipboard and followed Evan out of the room. As he strode across the open quadrangle, he thought of what had been going on with Toad Clark. He had heard rumors that several upperclassmen were giving him hell because he resembled an actor who starred in a movie about the first Black cadet at an all-White military college in South Carolina. In the movie, the actor had been threatened and harassed as the other cadets tried to coerce him to leave the college. Because Toad Clark resembled the actor (and he really did), the cadets were making some of the same hateful, racist, prejudiced comments and remarks as in the movie. Often the incidents would leave Toad Clark in a fit of rage or in tears. By now, however, Jon had had enough of the bullshit! In one of the recent BSA meetings, he had told everyone that if they saw or heard anything which was racist, in poor taste, prejudiced, or off-color, they were to tell one of the BSA officers immediately.

As Jon approached the "H" company formation, followed by several members of the BSA, he saw three cadets standing around Toad Clark in the rear of the formation. The three cadets were yelling at the toad. Yelling so hard, in fact, that their faces were beet red. One cadet was at each ear, and one in front. Toad Clark stood there bracing and shaking.

Jon walked up to the mini-formation and stopped. One of the cadets, noticing him, nudged one of the other cadets and turned to face Jon. The other two cadets stepped to the side of the cadet who noticed Jon first.

It was now quiet all over the barracks. Jon was aware that all eyes in the barracks were on him. He looked at the three cadets with an icy glare. His eyes finally rested upon the one he was sure was the ringleader. Jon looked at him for a moment then looked down at his clipboard and chuckled.

"What's the matter, boys, you don't have enough to eat, so you have to mess with my meat?"

There was silence as the three cadets looked contemptuously at Jon. One cadet, with his lip full of dip, spit on the ground next to Jon's shoes.

Jon, fixing an icy glare on the ringleader, took a step forward and brought his face to within inches of the ringleader's. He stared at him and then without removing his eyes barked a command to Clark.

"Get to formation, Clark!"

"Sir, Yes, Sir!"

Clark scurried past the cadets and ran happily to his formation. After a long pause, Jon addressed the three cadets.

"Look, gentlemen, I'm not sure what was going on here, but whatever—"

"Your damn toad didn't ask—" began one of the three cadets.

"Shut the fuck up!" roared Dwayne, one of the BSA members.

"As I was saying," continued Jon calmly, "whatever it was, it was not necessary to—"

"You don't know that!" snarled the ringleader.

"Again, as I was saying, it was not necessary to detain him. If you have a problem with one of my toads, you come see me," Jon said, ignoring the ringleader's comment. "I would do the same if I had a problem with one of yours. But I think we all know it is deeper than that, don't we?"

"We don't know what the hell you are talking about," said the third cadet defiantly.

"After mess tonight, I will be having a conversation with your company commander. I am sure it is more than just the three of you who have been harassing Clark with all your fucked-up little racist, prejudiced threats and remarks. So, if threats are what you respond to, try this one on for size. If I ever hear, or see, or catch you fucking with one of my toads, much less threatening or making any racial, prejudiced remarks to one, I'll personally visit each one of you and stick my foot so far up your ass, that you'll be shittin' shoestrings and burping polish for a month! Do we understand each other?" Jon paused for effect. "I'm sure we do!"

Having finished what he was saying, and not interested in their responses, Jon wheeled around and walked away slowly. The remaining BSA members stood motionless for a moment, glaring at the three cadets. Then, one by one, they walked away. Moments later, over at his own formation, the BSA members addressed Jon.

"Are you going to have the Assassin 'visit' with those three tonight?" asked one of the BSA members.

"Nah, not yet. Wait and see what happens with their company commander tonight. If he doesn't act right, then I will contact him and 'the fellas'.

"Cool. All you gotta do is ring his bell and he'll ring theirs!"

"Well, if they don't act right, I'll do just that. You just make sure you and the fellas are always ready!"

"And you think we're not? Shiiiiit!"

In the formation, Clark was standing next to another Black classmate. Jon gave him a nudge of approval, and they both smiled.

Later that night, Jon, Theo, and Evan walked up the stairs and down the corridor to the "H" company commander's room. Evan knocked on the door. A second later, a White cadet with red hair and a medium build appeared at the door.

"Yeah?"

"We need to speak to your company commander," said Theo.

"Yeah, he's been expectin' you," said the red-haired cadet as he pushed open the screen door and motioned for the cadets to enter. "Come on in."

He pointed toward the corner of the room where several dressers and full presses were lined up in a semi-formation.

"He's over there."

Jon, Theo, and Evan walked through the maze to the corner. The company commander sat leaning back in his chair with his feet up on his desk. He had a dip of snuff in his lip and was holding a spit cup in his left hand. The cup was browned and dirty on the inside.

What a gross, disgusting habit, thought Jon.

The company commander put the cup up to his lips and spit, then looked up and gave a wide, disarming smile.

"What can I do for you boys?"

"I am sure you heard about what happened tonight in your evening formation," said Theo.

"Yep, shore did," said the company commander, shaking his head in disgust.

"Well, this isn't the first time it happened. It has been going on for some time now. We just happened to catch it tonight," said Theo.

"Well, you know what they say. It ain't a crime until you get caught," said the company commander, smiling and spitting into his cup.

Jon, Theo, and Evan stared at the senior cadet, unamused. The company commander stopped smiling, took his feet off his desk, and returned the chair to its normal position.

"How do you know it has been going on for a while?"

"Because your cadets admitted to it," said Theo.

"All we want is for it to stop. For a message to be sent," said Evan.

"Message? What sort of message?" said the company commander, again, spitting into his cup.

"A message that that kind of behavior will not be tolerated," said Evan.

"Aw, c'mon guys, this is college, and boys will be boys. They were just havin' a little fun. There was no harm done!"

"That is not our idea of fun," said Theo angrily.

"Well, we're in college too, and our idea of having fun is not racial harassment. We are supposed to be M.U.T.S. men, not boys," said Evan, sarcastically.

"This was not just havin' fun," said Jon. "This was malicious and cruel. We want a message sent. Are you prepared to send that message or are we gonna have to speak to someone else?"

"Well, that won't be necessary," said the company commander, finally getting serious. "Awright, what do you want?"

"Ten confinements, the loss of rank, and an end to the bullshit. For any subsequent offense, ten promenades and the loss of rank," said Jon.

"That's a bit much, don't you think?"

"No!"

"How about five confinements and a stiff warning?"

"How about ten?"

"C'mon, fellas! You're squeezin' my balls kinda tight here!"

Jon stared at the company commander intently.

"Oh, awright, I'll give each one of them ten confinements. But I will not strip them of their ranks"!"

"We appreciate your cooperation, Sir," said Jon. "We'll expect to see them on the Punishment List this week."

Jon turned and walked out of the room quickly, followed by Theo and Evan.

The three filed out onto the noisy corridor. Freshman cadets scurried around sweeping and mopping the concrete corridor outside the cadet's rooms in the barracks. Upperclassmen ran after them, yelling threats and barking orders. Sweep Detail was always so chaotic.

The three cadets walked down the stairs without saying a word. After crossing to the other side of the barracks, Evan broke the silence.

"Well, whaddya think? Was that enough? Only ten confinements. I don't think that was enough. What do you think, Theo?"

"I think it was a battle won, that's what I think."

"Well, I think a little bit of something is better than a whole lot of nothing. You gotta crawl before you can walk. This is gonna be a long year. We better take what we can get for now," said Jon.

Jon looked around the barracks at the chaos. He then looked at his two friends and smiled.

"Yep, it's gonna be a long year, and we won't always be so lucky."

CHAPTER 6

J on sat at his desk working on the homework from his constitutional law class. He really enjoyed this class! Jon recalled when he signed up for the class and how he thought that constitutional law would be so boring. Boy was he pleasantly surprised! The class turned out to be both interesting and informative. He actually looked forward to going each week. He supposed that his enjoyment of the class, combined with his growing interest in the class, made the "A" he was currently getting understandable.

While Jon sat, totally absorbed in his work, there was a sudden loud thud at his door.

"Sir, Mr. Quest, Sir, request permission to enter!"

"Granted! Get in here!"

Jon's door flew open and a company "runner" quickly entered. He located Jon's full press and positioned himself in front of it, being careful to place his heels against the bottom rim. Once positioned, he stood there bracing, out of breath, and sweating.

The company "runner" was a toad who was at the disposal of the company clerks each morning from 7:15 am to 7:45 am and each evening from 10:30 pm to 11:00 pm. They ran all errands necessary for company clerks, company first sergeants, company executive officers, and company commanders. They delivered paperwork, messages, etc. When acting in the capacity of a company runner, a toad did not have to salute officers or abide by many of the rules for non-running toads. In order to be identified as company runners, toads were required to dress in black M.U.T.S. shorts, gold M.U.T.S. t-shirts, sneakers, and black socks. In the winter, they wore the black and gold jogging suits. During the toad year, every toad had to be a company runner at least two times. The impressive and sharp toads often saw company runner duty several times.

"Sir, Mr. Quest, Sir, Mr. McFadden wants to see you in his room, asap, Sir!"

"Why?"

"Sir, no excuse, Sir."

Jon got out of his chair and walked over to the toad. He stood directly in front of him and looked into his eyes. His face was solemn.

"You have no clue as to why?"

"Sir, no excuse, Sir."

"C'mon, I know you know or overheard something," Jon said jokingly. "What's it about?"

"Sir, it's about what happened in evening formation and you going to talk to the 'H' company commander, Sir."

"See, you know more than you think you do and more than you admit to, don't you?"

"Sir, yes, Sir," said the toad, smiling.

"Awright, what else?"

"Sir, nothing, Sir."

"Okay, then, beat it."

"Sir, Mr. Quest, Sir, it was certainly my pleasure to have been in the presence of a talented and modest human being such as yourself. However, Sir, because I am not worthy of such pleasure, I respectfully request your permission to remove my lowly, protoplasmic mass from your highly exalted presence, Sir!"

"Granted."

Jon chuckled as the toad ran out of his room. Each junior or senior who held the rank of platoon sergeant or above had the luxury of customizing what they wanted toads to say to them upon exiting their rooms or their messes. Jon created what he wanted the toads to say and chuckled every time he heard it recited.

Who would have thought an eighteen-year-old White man would have to say something like that to a twenty-year-old Black man, in the South!

Jon stretched, glanced at his watch, then looked around his room for his slippers. He spotted them under the edge of the racks. He walked over and slipped them on. He walked over to the door, opened it, then paused. He normally never left his room without letting someone know where he was going. Tyrone, his roommate, had not come back from studying yet. Therefore, Jon walked back to his desk and wrote him a note telling him he was going to talk to "little red riding hood," as he referred to his company commander. After dropping the note on Tyrone's rack, he headed for Stan McFadden's room.

Stan McFadden was Jon's company commander. He never liked Jon. When Jon was a freshman, Stan constantly harassed him. When Jon was a sophomore, the contempt was present, but mostly masked. Stan, a red head with a slight build, was responsible for Jon not making a higher rank than Platoon Sergeant his junior year. Jon believed Stan took his name off the rank boards and "black-balled" him. There was no love lost between Jon and Stan.

Jon opened the screen and walked into Stan's room, pausing momentarily to knock loudly on the door. Stan was sitting at his desk in the comer.

"You wanted to see me, Stan?"

Without looking up, Stan motioned Jon to a chair next to his desk.

"No thanks, I'd rather stand. I'm sure whatever this is about, it won't take long."

"Suit yourself."

Stan continued to sift through a stack of papers on his desk, without answering. Jon stood there silently for a moment.

"You wanted to see me?" he repeated.

"Yeah, yeah."

Stan collected the papers and tapped them on the desk. He then looked up at Jon.

"I heard you went to see 'H' company commander, this evening."

"Yeah, and . . ."

"Well, I think you're getting too big for your britches! If you have a problem, you come to me, then I'll talk to the company commander, if I see fit!"

"Well, that's exactly what I'm afraid of. I don't trust you to 'see fit'!"

"Look, Mister, you skipped over the chain of command! You were supposed to—"

"I was supposed to do exactly what I did! I didn't go see him as a Kilo company Platoon Sergeant. I went to see him as the Black Students Association President. As the BSA President, I have the authority to talk to anyone, if it pertains to my association or the cadets in it."

"Don't you throw policy in my face, Mister," said Stan as his face turned red. "I know policy! I am tired of you, with your high and mighty attitude, just doing whatever the heck you please just because you're the president of some darn party group!"

"You done?"

"No, I'm not! I'll let you know when I'm done, Sergeant! I'm warning you, Quest, you better back off. You're pissing off a lot of people. You are ruining your career here. You're ruining your chance at a high rank next year—"

"I think you've already taken care of that for me," Jon interrupted, sarcastically.

"You're ruining your chance at good grades and jeopardizing your chance at graduating," continued Stan.

"Is that a threat?"

"No, it's a warning!"

"May I be dismissed . . . Sir?" Jon said, bristling.

Stan, who was now positioned a few feet in front of Jon, stared hard, infuriated.

"Yes, you can, Sergeant. But I'd advise you to heed my warnings!"

"Thank you for your concern, Sir," Jon said sardonically as he exited Stan's room.

Back on the corridor, Jon let out a loud sigh.

"Fuck you!" Jon said aloud as he walked down the corridor toward his room.

CHAPTER 7

J on sat quietly as Adam conducted the bimonthly BSA meeting. His thoughts were far away from the present meeting. So much so that he hadn't heard anything that had been said in the room thus far.

Jon's thoughts were focused on the remainder of the first semester, specifically how he and the other officers of the BSA were going to stem the obvious tide of racism that was on the rise there at the M.U.T.S.

"Well, what are your thoughts on that, Jon?" asked Adam, turning to look at Jon.

"Jon!"

"Yeah, huh, what? Thoughts about what?"

"We were saying, we need to plan a party out at the beach house to raise some funds for our Family and Friends Day reception. What are your thoughts?"

"Oh, yeah, I think that's a great idea. The further out of the red we stay, the better. When are we talking?"

"We had not decided," said Adam, turning to the rest of the cadets.

Adam looked at the cadets, shrugged his shoulders, and extended his arms as he posed the question nonverbally.

"Well, I don't know about all of you, but I think we need one PDQ," responded Tommy.

"Shit, sooner than that," said Tyrone. "The other colleges are already on their second party."

The room suddenly was alive with chatter as the cadets discussed the "need" for a BSA beach party and the soonest possible date.

"Awright, awright," said Adam, holding his hands up to silence the group. "I'll go talk to Ms. Mueller and find out the soonest date that the beach house is available. Okay, that's all I have, so we'll close our meeting with comments from our Prez', Jon."

Jon rose and walked over to the window. He looked out of the window into the still darkness which had already settled like a fluffy blanket over the parade deck. For a moment, Jon became lost in the darkness. The darkness was so silent and still that it enveloped the nights and protected them from all the vulnerabilities which now trapped the days. In the darkness, people were released from running the usual frantic pace that characterized their days. The darkness provided both an invitation to slow down and rest, all the while giving the excuse necessary to give the body a much-needed break.

Jon's eyes moved through the darkness and rested upon the largest cadet barracks. The barracks were lit up and seemed full of life. This one barrack was a paradox to the deep darkness, just as M.U.T.S. was a paradox to the belief that times change. Jon turned around and faced the group. He leaned on the window ledge and surveyed his fellow cadets. These were the cadets who trusted and respected him. These were the cadets who had voted unanimously to elect him as the president of the BSA in his junior year. These were the cadets who expected his leadership to legitimize the BSA's status as a service organization. These were the cadets who expected his leadership to legitimately give the BSA a place among the other extracurricular organizations on that campus.

The cadets' high expectations laid great responsibility upon Jon's shoulders. This responsibility kept his mind racing with new ideas and effective solutions to their many problems. There was the problem of being in the red . . . severely in the red. There was the problem of the total lack of respect they received from the administration. The administration's lack of respect made approval for special programs and the money to fund them nonexistent.

Hell, if it were not for Dr. Annette Mueller, the director of cadet extra-curricular activities, we wouldn't have a prayer. Thank God for having a sistah in high places! Jon had thought on many occasions.

"Look, guys," said Jon, finally addressing the group, "we've got problems. There seems to be a resurgence of racism here. I have heard of more 'incidents' in the first month and a half of this year than I did all last year!"

"It was just as bad then," interjected Dwayne. "It's just that nobody talked about it. We all just dealt with it. I mean, we talked about it amongst ourselves, but no one ever had us talk about it and voice it in a meeting or anything. The only thing is that last year we would come to you in private. Everyone didn't know to do that. Everyone didn't know about you and 'the fellas'."

"Yeah, since you asked everyone to start communicating any comments or incidents, it is all coming out in the open," said another cadet.

"Yeah, well that is still disturbing because there is a major difference from last year and this year," continued Jon. "Last year it was pretty much the same basic people or companies. It was also the same kind of things, the comments, the jokes, and the ignorant behavior. This year, everything seems to have gone to a higher level. When anything goes unchecked long enough . . . Well, anyway, this year, instead of being a sopho-more secretary with the fellas, I am the junior president with the fellas, and therein lies the main difference. Last year, I had to clear everything and double-check or answer to someone, but not anymore! This year, we ain't gonna let this shit continue! I mean, I understand this is the South and this place has a lot of tradition, but we are Black men and we matter too," said Jon as he patted his chest with an open palm. "And I know that all of you feel like that!"

"So now the question becomes, what are we gonna do about it?" said McKenzie.

"Yeah, now that we're hearing all of this, we gotta do some-thin'," said Evan.

"You're all right, we do have to do something. But we have to be careful to do it the right way, or it will blow up in our faces," said Theo.

"Yeah, right! As if the shit ain't already in our faces," said Adam pointedly.

"Yeah, okay, Jon, what now?" inquired Albert. "We gonna let the fellas deal with all of this, or what?"

Jon looked at Albert. "Why do you think that would be of interest to them?" "I don't know, you'd have to ask them," said Albert.

"Hmmm, I just might."

Jon paused a moment and surveyed his audience.

"But then again, that would keep them too busy. There aren't enough nights in the year for the work they would have to do. But that's a moot point anyway. I only talk to them when they contact me. I wouldn't even know how to go about getting in touch with them."

Once again, Jon began smiling while he looked over his audience.

"If any of you do know how to get in touch with one of them, have them give me a call, would you? I'd just like to talk to them. I'd at least like to know who they are and how to get to them. Ya know? But the time would not be right for them to become active, at least not yet. We must play the game. We have to do it right, first. We have to go right to the top. Then, if going to the top doesn't work—"

"The top?" someone mumbled. "What top?"

"The regimental commander."

"The regimental commander?" several cadets said, almost in unison.

"Why would you go to that sorry-ass mutha fucka?" asked Tommy.

"Yeah, you know he ain't gonna do shit," said Tyrone.

"I mean, what you gonna say, 'Could you please stop all of your buddies from making my little niggas uncomfortable here at your bastion of the South, Sir?'"

"Good luck," murmured a disenchanted cadet in the rear of the room.

"We don't need good luck. What we need is to cover all our bases," said Jon. "And that is exactly what we're gonna do! We are gonna follow the chain of command. What we're gonna to do is shut them up later by giving them a chance to correct the problems now. We are gonna play the game. No, we are gonna win the game. If y'all don't learn anything else while I'm here, learn how to play and win the game. Don't fool yourselves, there is a game being played. We have to get in the game, learn the game, then win the game. We can't be afraid to play. Oh, yeah, we are gonna go to the regimental commander. We are gonna do the right thing. Me, and the other officers, are gonna go see the RC, this week. We are gonna make him aware of all the incidents which have occurred so far. We are gonna have it thoroughly documented and ready to place in his hand. We are gonna make a good faith attempt to let them resolve it their way. Then if they don't, we will resolve it our way!"

Jon turned to Nate, the BSA secretary.

"See to it that everything is documented and ready for me, asap!"

"No prob," said Nate.

"Then after we give him the report, we'll tell him what we want him to do about all of this," said Jon.

"Well, what do we want him to do?" asked Craig, one of the BSA freshmen.

"Fix the shit!" said Adam.

"No shit, Sherlock! But how?" asked Tyrone.

"Well, we're gonna tell him we want him to call a meeting with all his barracks commanders and tell them to call a meeting with each of their company commanders. We want them to explain to everyone the seriousness of the racial jokes and slurs. We want them to explain to everyone that they will not tolerate any racial harassment. We want them to tell them that any further reports will result in definite, swift, and severe punishment."

"Man, you think they'll do that?" asked one of the cadets in the group.

"Hell, no!" said Adam.

"Well, the point is not to pre-judge what they will do," said Jon. "The point is to give them the chance. Then if they do, fine. If they don't, then they have had their chance. But as my mama always says, 'Nothing beats a failure, but a try!'"

"In other words, they will have been warned," said Adam.

"Do you think the RC will meet with you?" asked Dwayne.

"Theo has already set up the appointment. He didn't have a choice," said Tim.

"We made him an offer he couldn't refuse," said Albert, smiling.

"Okay, Jon, when is the meeting?" asked McKenzie.

"Well, Nate will need to get me that documentation by the end of tomorrow because we meet with him and the Executive Officer on Thursday morning. I'll expect Theo, Adam, and Nate to accompany me to this meeting. Any problems with that, gentlemen?"

"None with me," said Theo.

"No prob," said Nate.

Adam, who was leaning back in his chair with his arms folded across his chest, sighed loudly.

"Well, I'll have to check my 'sheh-jool' . . . and I'll let you know."

"Like yo' ass would miss that meeting," remarked Albert.

"Awright guys, that's all I have. Oh. One last thing. Keep your eyes and ears open for any racial harassment. Pay close attention to our Black Toads. If you see anything, questionable or blatant, let one of us know. But don't stop there! Remember to also document everything! Encourage all your buddies who aren't here tonight to do the same. This is a new day. No longer are we steppin' and fetchin'! We belong here as much as anyone. It is our time to stand up and be strong Black men. It is our time to let them know this shit won't continue. The bullshit stops now!"

The other cadets nodded and vocally expressed their agreement with Jon's statements.

Jon felt great! These meetings, and other times like this, had always initiated such intense and powerful feelings for Jon. These times made him feel like there was still hope for having a positive college experience. It was in these times that Jon felt like he was part of something worthwhile. It was, in fact, a renaissance of sorts. There was a revival of hope emerging, and he was at the very center of the revival. Jon had always admired Martin Luther King Jr. and El-Hajj Malik El-Shabazz (Malcolm X) for their sense of purpose and the feeling of hope they gave.

There were others (John Lewis, Ella Baker, Medgar Evers, and Harriet Tubman, to name a few) whose methods may have been questioned by some but who had always held Jon's respect for their strong sense of purpose. Jon felt that he had the same mission. He felt he had the same purpose. He felt he had the same responsibility. It was a responsibility that Jon accepted with honor and humility. Jon had known from the time he arrived at M.U.T.S. that he would undoubtedly leave an impression on his college. He knew he would do something special there. Jon did not know if he would leave M.U.T.S. famous or infamous. But he knew his goal was to be a role model to others and to pave the way for others behind him. Jon always knew this would involve him making sacrifices and would require him sticking his neck out. He felt that a man was not anything if he had not found something in life worth working for and sacrificing that very life for. If no such thing had been discovered, then he had not yet lived; he had merely existed. Jon would not merely exist. Life was too short, and the plight of the Black community was too important!

It all starts here, Jon had often thought. *It starts with the Black youth. If we would readjust and refocus ourselves, then we could position ourselves to truly make a difference. It is not all about wearing the kente cloth, the kufis, the "X" shirts, or the Africa medallions. It is not all about saying "I own my own company" if that company is not making it. It is not about any of that because we are too talented to be so limited. If we can run major departments and be the brains behind major companies, then we should not settle for mediocrity or less. It is almost as if just owning it is enough, but it is not! It is not all about just owning. It's about recognizing that as long as we don't work together, as long as we treat each other like second-class citizens, as long as we continue to measure ourselves by someone else's ruler, then we will always play catch-up and will never quite measure up.*

We have to break the chains of mental slavery and escape the psychological bondage in which we have been placed. The only way to do that is to band together, combine our strengths, fortify our weaknesses, and come forth! We must start with teaching our young people these lessons. Our young people must move from underneath the title of the "Me Generation." That title was not created by a Black. It does not describe how we should be or used to be. That title does however describe how they want us to be. If they keep us focused on "getting mine," then we won't be able to focus on all of us "getting ours." There is strength in numbers, even when those numbers are trying to fight or reach economic stability and prosperity. Oh, the miseducation and misdirection that we as a race have been exposed to!

Jon had gotten lost in his thoughts again. The plight of Black America had always been a passionate subject for him.

"Awright, gentlemen," Jon said, finally addressing the group again. "Our next meeting is in two weeks. Same Black channel, same Black time. And remember, come back Black, or don't come back! Peace."

There was immediate conversation around the room as the cadets gathered their books, hats, and other belongings.

Several cadets came over to talk to Jon. They talked about various incidents they had seen, heard, or to which they had been exposed. They talked about the BSA party. They talked about the Family Day reception. One cadet, in particular, pulled Jon away from the others.

"Jon, I want you to meet someone," said Ellis.

Ellis was Jon's fraternity brother. They had "crossed the sands of immortality" together. They were relatively close and made it a point of eyeing all the new cadets to see who was worthy to join them within the ranks of the elite.

Ellis, a senior, was very excitable and made it a point of letting everyone know that he and the BSA President were close.

So much so that he often played up their relationship in order to make himself appear more important.

Ellis pulled a cadet toward him by his shoulder. The cadet, who reluctantly allowed himself to be maneuvered, peered sheepishly at Jon through a pair of unsightly eyeglasses.

"This is Brent Hansen. He is the brother of Barden Hansen. You know the guy that's on the board of the school. Brent, this is Jon Quest. Get to know him. He is the most influential Black cadet on the yard. He's my frat, so if you just stick close to me, you'll be alright. Jon, I think Brent may be a candidate," said Ellis as he patted Brent on the back.

"Well, great! Brent, it is a pleasure to meet you. I see you're in the same company as Ellis. That's great. If you need anything, he's the man to see. Adam, our VP, is also in your barracks. So, keep in touch with those two and you'll be alright."

Jon looked at the freshman, who wore a puzzled look on his face.

"What's the problem?" asked Jon.

"Sir, who is Adam, Sir?"

"Oh, that's right," chuckled Jon. "You don't know us by our first names. . . yet."

Jon looked around the room and spotted Adam talking to a group of cadets near the door.

"Hey, Adam," yelled Jon.

"Yeah," said Adam as he looked around to see who was calling him.

"C'mere a sec."

Adam said his goodbyes and strode over to Jon.

"Whassup?"

"I want you to meet Brent Hansen. He is the—"

"Brother of Barden Hansen. Yeah, I know all about him. I already peeped him out in the barracks. I been watching him.

He's been taking a lot of shit, too. I guess because of who his brother is."

"Well, you never cease to amaze me! I'm glad to know you have been watchin'. Trust me, Brent, there is no better man to watch your back than this one," said Jon as he patted Adam on the shoulder. "He's always on the ball. Look, Brent, if things get too tough or if they really start fucking with you too bad, you go straight to Adam. If anything, out of line happens, anything at all, we want to know. We don't want them dancing on that thin line between harassment and toad treatment. I'm serious. You got me?"

"Sir, yes, Sir," said Brent as he stiffened.

The upper-class cadets looked at each other and laughed.

"Relax, Brent. Here you're among friends," said Ellis.

"Yeah, it's out there you have to worry about," said Adam, pointing toward the window.

"All right guys, I gotta break. I got a test I need to study for," said Jon as he bent down and began collecting his things.

Afterward, Jon walked to the door, stopped, and turned to address the remaining cadets in the room.

"Gentlemen remember what we talked about," he said, loudly. "I'm outta here . . . seeeeeee yaaa!"

Jon turned and walked down the hall to a chorus of goodbyes. He walked down the steps and slipped his overseas cap onto his head. At the bottom of the steps he paused for a moment as he heard an outbreak of laughter from upstairs. Jon then walked out of the building and into the darkness.

CHAPTER 8

The phone in Jon's room had rung only once. The sudden ring came as a short, quick burst. Jon immediately recognized that ring. If the phone rang for two successive short rings, the call was coming from off campus. However, if the ring was a short, quick burst, the call was coming from somewhere on campus. This information had been especially helpful for Jon. Since he had become an upperclassman, Jon had been allowed to have a telephone; however, he had received obscene phone calls. Therefore, the ring from the phone had always let him know if the enemy dwelled within or without.

Jon, who had been working on homework from his international law class, looked at the clock on his desk. It was 8:36 pm. After the third ring, Jon picked up the handset.

"Platoon Sergeant Quest," said Jon in his usual nonchalant, semi-monotone voice.

"Hey, Jon, er, what's up?"

Jon recognized Theo's voice immediately.

"Hey, Theo, nothin' much."

"Jus' callin' to let you know that, er, the meeting with the regimental commander has been moved. Instead of tomorrow morning after breakfast, it has been moved to tomorrow night after evening mess. Is that okay?"

"Yeah, that's great. It will give us more time. Do me a favor and call Adam and Nate and let them know about the change. Tell them to meet us in my room right after second rest. By the way, tell Nate to send all the copies over to my room tonight at 10:30, so I can review them. Also, have him send copies over to Adam so he can review them as well."

"Will do."

"Awright, cuz."

Jon hung up the phone and sat motionless for a moment. After a few minutes, Tyrone, who was sitting at his desk, turned, and addressed Jon.

"Sooo . . .? Whassup?"

"Oh nothin'. We meet with the regimental commander tomorrow night instead of tomorrow mornin'."

"Good luck! You know he's a little bitch. He probably needs more time to get ready for you."

"Yeah, I'm sure."

Jon was already a hundred miles away. He was thinking about the meeting. He knew he would catch hell from Stan. He would probably catch hell from everyone, except the bruthas.

"Hmmmmm," he said aloud as he thought about catching hell. A lot of guys out there tried to fuck with Jon. If they tried to fuck with him, he knew they had tried to fuck with the other Black cadets.

"Ya know, Tyrone," Jon said, slowly. "Do you remember when we were in the meeting the other night and Albert brought up the issue of having 'the fellas' to start with more of these racial issues?"

"Yeah. Yeah, I do," said Tyrone, turning to look at his roommate.

"How does that sound to you?"

"Yo, that shit sounds fly to me," said Tyrone, excitedly.

"Yeah it does, doesn't it?" said Jon thoughtfully.

"So, what's your point? What's up?" Tyrone demanded anxiously.

Jon laughed as he looked at his roommate. Tyrone was standing in front of Jon, with eyes sparkling, and a huge grin.

"Boy, I'll tell you what! You jokers from D.C. think you smell a little blood and you're on it, huh?!"

"Hell, yeah!!!"

"So, what's up? I know you well enough to know that you don't waste your time with idle thoughts. Somethin' is brewing. I've heard those wheels in your head turning all night. What . . . is . . .up!" demanded Tyrone, again.

"Don't worry about it. When, and if, the time is right, I'll let you know. Until then, not a word to anyone. I have to protect you from knowing too much. The day will come when they will come after you because of me. When that day does come, I don't want you to know too much. It will be much easier if you aren't lying when you say that I did not tell you very much. It's for your own protection."

"But I do know some things."

"True. But that which you know comes from overhearing phone calls and conversations. I try to keep you out of the loop as much as I can. If something were to happen to you because of me, I don't think I could forgive myself. You're muh frat, muh boy, and muh room dog and I don't want those things to be your downfall. So, you have to make sure you keep everything you hear to yourself. You can't tell anybody. The day may come when they ask you what you know. I want you to be able to say nothing and not have someone else come back and say you told them something. Or I don't want someone to say they know you know because of something you told somebody which got back to them. So, the easiest way is just not to tell anybody!"

"Not even my . . ."

"Especially not her! She'll tell one of her girls, who will tell one of her girls, and so on, and so on. Next thing you know . . . badda boom, badda bing, the entire world knows. You know how women are."

"Yeah, awright," said Tyrone, his obvious disappointment showing. "Incidentally, I wanted to tell you something. Remember the other night at the meeting . . .?"

"Yeah. What about it?"

"All that talk you did about 'I don't know how to get in touch with the fellas, and if anyone knows, tell them this and that. I have to wait for them to contact me. I don't know who they are.' Man, why you stand up there, looking all innocent and tell them lies. Like you don't know shit? Like you weren't the one who put the fellas together in the first place! Man, you are a bad mutha fucka!"

"How do you know I was lying?" asked Jon facetiously.

Tyrone studied Jon a moment. Jon sat straight-faced, looking at Tyrone. For a moment, Tyrone was confused. Then catching himself, he smiled.

"Yeah, right!"

Jon and Theo sat together in Jon's room. As the two waited for Adam and Nate to join them, they discussed the strategy for the evening.

"Theo, since you are a senior officer, I'll let you start off talking. I am expecting there to be three or four of them there. Tell them who we are, who we represent, and then let them know we are there to discuss some very serious issues with them. Now, after you let them know these things, tell them that I will get into more detail. At that time, I—"

Suddenly, there was a loud noise as someone began beating the screen against the door.

"Sir, Mr. Quest, Sir, Company Runner reporting as ordered, Sir!"

Jon looked at Theo in bewilderment.

"Company Runner? I didn't send for a company runner."

Theo, looking at Jon, shrugged his shoulders.

"Maybe Stan sent him," said Theo.

"Yeah, maybe," agreed Jon. "Get in here!" he yelled.

The door flew open and a freshman cadet rushed into Jon's room. He quickly found the full press and positioned his heels against the bottom edge and stood there, bracing.

Jon looked at the toad standing there and sweating. He was dressed in black gym shorts and a gold T-shirt with the M.U.T.S. insignia on the left breast.

"You better not drip any sweat on my floor," Jon said as he winked at Theo.

Once again, there was a loud noise as someone banged Jon's screen up against his door.

"Boy, are you popular tonight," said Theo.

"Sir, Mr. Quest, Sir, Cadet . . ."

At that time, the cadet's voice became muffled and indistinguishable. ". . . reporting as ordered, Sir!"

"Who did they say?" Jon asked Theo.

"I couldn't tell."

Jon turned to the toad already in his room.

"Who did they say they were, Toad?"

"Sir, no excuse, Sir."

"You couldn't tell either?"

"Sir, no, Sir."

Once again, the screen door banged loudly against the door.

"Sir, Mr. Quest, Sir, Cadet . . ."

Once again Jon could not make out the name. ". . . reporting as ordered, Sir!"

Jon could not recall telling anyone to come to his room. He had not really even talked to any of the freshmen. He knew he would not have told anyone to come by tonight, especially since he knew he had a meeting with the regimental commander. Then it dawned on him who was at his door.

"Get in here, maggot!"

The door was once again thrown open, and Adam and Nate rushed in. They ran into the room feigning a brace. They ran around in circles, bumping into each other and the others in the room. Finally, after shoving the "true" toad out of the way, the two lined up their heels with the edge of the full press and stood at attention.

"Sir, Mr. Quest, Sir, cadets Bad Dream and Wet Dream reporting as ordered, Sir," said Adam.

Jon, Theo, the "true" toad, Adam, and Nate all laughed.

After exchanging greetings consisting of the customary "whassup" and handshakes, Jon turned to the toad.

"Now, what do you want?"

"Sir, Mr. Quest, Sir, Mr. McFadden wants to see you ASAP, Sir."

"Oh, yeah?" said Jon, looking at his fellow BSA members. "Well tell him I'll be there in a little bit."

"Sir?" the toad said with uncertainty.

"You heard me! Tell him I will be there in a little while!"

"Sir, Mr. Quest, Sir, it is certainly my—"

"Yeah, yeah, yeah. Out, out, out!"

The toad ran quickly out of Jon's room.

"Told ya," said Theo, smiling at Jon.

"As always, you were right," Jon said, bowing to Theo.

"Yo man, where's Tyrone?" asked Nate.

"You know that mutha fucka ain't leavin' the mess hall until they put his ass out," laughed Jon.

The others joined in on the laugh.

"Awright, y'all ready?"

"Yep."

"Yeah."

"Let's do it."

"Adam, I'll give you a chance to talk after Theo opens up. Nate, you just follow our lead. There should be no need for you to say anything. After Theo opens, Adam and I will do the talking, okay?"

The other three cadets nodded in agreement.

"Nate, do you have the copies for the regimental commander?"

"Yeah, right here," he said, patting the portfolio case he always carried.

"How many copies did you prepare?"

"Well, you have one. Adam has one. I have one in here just in case either of you two lost or misplaced yours, and I have seven more copies."

"Excellent! I have my copies. Adam, did you bring yours?"

"Yep, got 'em right here," said Adam, holding up a leather binder.

"Well then," said Jon as he walked toward his door. "Let's do it."

Jon walked out of his door, followed by the other three cadets. They walked down the corridor and up three flights of steps to the third floor. At the top of the stairs, they turned left and walked toward the regimental commander's room. As they walked, they quietly discussed details and incidents.

Upon arriving at the regimental commander's room, they arranged themselves into a military file: Theo, a senior officer, in front; Jon, a junior platoon sergeant, next; Adam, a junior squad sergeant, third; and Nate, a sophomore corporal, last.

Theo knocked on the door and they awaited a response.

"Come in," someone inside the room yelled.

The four officers from the BSA walked into the regimental commander's room.

The regimental commander's room was very large and overlooked the parade deck. Inside, the regimental commander, his roommate, and two other officers were sitting, facing the door. In front of them sat three chairs, obviously intended for Jon and only two others. Jon really liked being unpredictable.

Jon, Theo, Adam, and Nate walked to the three chairs and stopped. No one said a word.

Jon looked at each of the four White cadets. The regimental commander sat in the middle. To his immediate right was his roommate, the regimental executive officer. To the immediate left of the regimental commander sat another officer whom Jon recognized as the regimental provost marshal. The last cadet, who sat next to the regimental executive officer, Jon did not recognize.

The regimental commander spoke first.

"Good evening, gentlemen. Please have a seat."

Jon, Theo, and Adam sat down as Nate walked to the corner of the room to retrieve another chair. He picked the chair up, walked over, and placed it in the space behind Jon and Adam.

"I apologize, we only thought there were three of you coming," said the regimental commander, looking at Theo.

"No problem," said Theo.

"I must admit, when we were approached about this meeting, we were quite confused. We didn't understand why you wanted to talk to us. I mean, you have a company commander, a TAC officer, and a chain of command. At any rate, Theo here persuaded us to at least give you an audience . . . so, what can we do for you?"

"Well, er, first of all," began Theo, "we would like to, er, thank you for agreeing to see us. We realize you are busy and, er, you certainly could have told us to use our chain of command and left it there. However, er, as you will see, your agreeing to see us is a wise move. If we could have gone to the company commanders, we would have. However, the issues which we have to discuss, er, with you are bigger than one company. They involve the entire Corps of Cadets. Before we get into that, however, I must introduce you to the other cadets who are here with me. The four of us represent, er, the Black Students Association—"

"We are aware of that," the regimental executive officer interjected.

"At any rate," Theo continued, "first is Jon Quest, the president of the BSA. Next, is, er, Adam Terreaux, the vice president, and Nate Byrd, the secretary. I am the business manager for the, er, organization. At this time, I will turn it over to Jon, who will discuss why we are here."

"Thank you, Theo," Jon said as he smoothly accepted the baton Theo had so eloquently carried for the first leg. "Gentlemen, we are not here to bore you or waste your time. The very fact that we are here suggests a serious situation which is looming. We are here to implore your assistance in helping us deal with the situation."

"What situation is this, to which you refer?" asked the regimental commander, obviously puzzled.

"First of all, let me preface my comments by saying that everything I will be discussing with you is documented, factual, and in the records of the Black Students Association. This year, there seems to be, and in fact exists, a serious problem with a resurgence of racism here at the M.U.T.S."

The four White cadets became immediately and noticeably uncomfortable.

They shifted in their chairs and looked around at each other.

Jon realized that from this point forward, he had better talk fast, as his time was now limited. Jon also realized that no other

Black cadet had ever approached a regimental commander with an issue such as the racism which existed within the corps.

"We have several documented incidents, which range from telling racially offensive jokes to outright racial harassment."

"Now, Cadet Quest," interrupted the regimental commander, "you have documented proof of someone who was forced to listen to or take part in racially offensive jokes?"

"Yes, we do," said Jon as he motioned to Nate to give him the copies. Jon gathered the papers and held them out for the regimental commander.

"I don't need to see those," snapped the regimental commander. "I just asked you a question."

Then catching himself, he replied, "The providing of documentation is not necessary at this time. This is not the Honor Court. I am sure you all do believe what is on those papers. However, there are two sides to every story, and I am sure this is just being blown out of proportion—"

"Or is just a big misunderstanding," interjected the regimental executive officer.

"No, this is not a misunderstanding," replied Adam, "this is people being racially insensitive and offensive. This is people stepping out of line. This is some of the cadets taking this school too seriously!"

"I think you have a point," said the regimental executive officer coolly. "It is some cadets. It is not the entire corps, therefore, what has all of that got to do with us?"

"We would like you to stem the flow," said Adam.

"Excuse me," said the regimental commander, confused.

"We would like you to call a meeting with your barracks commanders and explain the seriousness of what is going on. We would like you to have them call a meeting with their entire barracks and address the problem. They should let them know that the jokes, comments, and harassment have got to stop. Additionally, any behavior will be met with swift and sure punishment. If you were to do this, this would stop this from getting out of control and it would send a clear message to the perpetrators, as well as the victims, that this kind of behavior will not be tolerated," Jon concluded.

"I don't really think that is a good idea," began the regimental commander. "I mean it would call attention to the issue. Therefore, there would be more people doing it because we brought it up. It would be like opening Pandora's box. No, I don't really think there is a problem. However, if we did something like that, there would be. It sounds to me like these are a few isolated incidents. I mean, c'mon guys, these are just some good ole boys having a little college fun!"

"Well, we don't think it is fun," sneered Adam. "I know these boys are M.U.T.S., but right now they are being Bad Dogs."

"Look," said Theo, "all we're asking is that you make a stand and let the corps know that this type of behavior is inappropriate and unacceptable."

"Well, gentlemen, I don't really see the need to continue this conversation. I appreciate you coming by, but we must wrap this up. We all have studying to do," said the regimental commander as he stood up.

The other three White cadets, following the lead of the regimental commander, also stood.

Jon, however, did not move. He sat motionless for a moment. The other Black cadets watched him intently to see what they should do. They remained still and silent. The silence in the room seemed to last for an hour.

Finally, Jon, eyes straight ahead, broke the silence. When he spoke, his voice was firm and determined.

"You gave us this audience and I would appreciate you sitting down until we are finished. We have studying to do, as well. I am sure we are as anxious to get out of here as you are to have us out, Sir."

The regimental commander looked around at the White cadets, then at the Black cadets, and finally at Jon. He smiled, wryly, and sat down. The other White cadets did the same.

"I am going to repeat myself again," said Jon, staring coldly at the regimental commander. "We want you to meet with your barracks commanders and have them meet with their barracks. We want them to tell their barracks that there is a lot of racial insensitivity going on in the corps, in the form of jokes, comments, and blatant harassment. We want them to tell everyone that it must stop. If it does not stop, there will be swift and sure consequences. If you do this, this will call attention to a snowballing problem. If you don't do this, the snowball will grow and pick up speed. If that happens, then before this year is out, there will be a major racial incident which will rock the college down to its very foundation. That is not a threat, nor a promise. It is a fact!"

Jon stood up, followed by Adam, Nate, and Theo. Jon surveyed the White cadets' expressions. The four White cadets sat there in a stupor. Jon tossed a copy of the documentation on the regimental commander's desk and turned to leave. Halfway into his turn, Jon stopped, and without looking at the regimental commander, addressed him.

"Will that be all, Sir?" Jon said stiffly.

Without waiting for an answer, Jon proceeded to the door. Nate stood, holding the door open. Adam and Theo already stood in the corridor, waiting for Jon to exit the regimental commander's room.

As Jon walked through the door, he issued one last address to the four White cadets.

"Remember what I said. Heed my warnings. It will be much easier to do this now than to deal with the consequences if you don't!"

Nate closed the door behind Jon and followed him out into the corridor.

As the four walked down the corridor, Stan approached the group. Adam and Nate positioned themselves between Stan and Jon. As Stan tried to maneuver between the two, Adam stepped in front of him. Whichever way Stan moved, Adam would cut him off, thereby not allowing him to come within arm's reach of Jon.

Stan, who had already appeared irritated, was now almost beside himself with anger.

He paused, took a deep breath, glared at Adam, then Nate, and finally, Jon.

"Excuse me," said Stan through clenched teeth, "I need to talk to Quest."

"Yeah? You and everybody else," replied Adam.

"What do you want, Stan?" said Jon with a sigh.

"I need to see you in my room, now!"

"Sorry, Stan, I can't. I've got a lot of studying to do. Maybe in the morning," Jon said lightly.

Jon turned and walked down the corridor with Theo at his side. Nate and Adam stood there momentarily glaring at Stan before following behind Jon. Stan stood for a moment, watching them in amazement. He looked at Jon as he walked down the corridor. Stan then looked at Adam. Adam returned the look and smiled a wide, toothy grin. Stan then turned away and loudly stormed off in the opposite direction.

Back in his room, Jon sat wearily at his desk.

"Well?" inquired Nate.

"All we can do is try, and we did just that! What we have to do now is try to keep ourselves intact. We obviously know we don't have their support, so we're on our own. It's always good to know who your enemies are and who you can really count on."

The four cadets each exchanged their views on how they thought the meeting went, with each cadet recapping the story from his own vantage point to one another and to Tyrone. At the end of the stories, Tyrone, who had been lying in his bed, raised up on his elbow.

"Fuck that," said Tyrone, angrily. "You guys should have cussed them mutha fuckas out before you left. Damn, that pisses me off!"

"Tyrone, I always tell you that you should never get emotional, it clouds your judgment," said Jon. "Hey, no big deal, tho'. Now we know. Next week we'll meet and talk about where we go from here. In the meantime, do not talk about what went on tonight to anyone until after the meeting. No need in stirring up the pot until we are ready to deal with all of it. I have some ideas on what we need to do as an organization. Adam, you, and I will discuss that later. But right now, you guys better get back to your rooms."

Adam, Theo, and Nate walked slowly and reluctantly toward the door.

"Hey," said Jon, "thanks! I appreciate your support. I appreciate everything. I really do. Adam, when you get back to Four, call the Assassin and tell him I want to see him, tonight. Tell him to meet you and me at 10:30 on the 'O' course. After you do that, call me, I want to talk to you about something."

Adam gave a crafty smile. "No problem consider it done! Talk to you soon."

The three cadets walked out of Jon's room and closed the door behind them. Jon sat in his chair quietly. Tyrone, now at his desk, sat angrily mumbling to himself. Jon, however, did not notice. He sat with a smile on his face, anticipating his 10:30 meeting with Adam and the Assassin.

CHAPTER 9

R ing!!! Ring!!!! Ring!!!!!
Jon scrambled from his top rack and groped in the dark for the telephone.

"Yeah?" said Jon sleepily, squinting his eyes as he tried to bring his clock into focus.

"Jon, this is Adam".

Jon could tell by the sound of Adam's voice that he was very upset.

"Yeah, whassup?" sighed Jon as he leaned on the side of his rack and rested his head on his forearm.

"Man, some serious shit just went down! I mean some fucked-up, heavy shit!"

"Some shit so fucked up and heavy that you had to call me at . . ." Jon paused and looked once again at the clock radio which rested on the top shelf of his desk. ". . . two thirty in the fuckin' mornin'?"

"Look, Jon, fuck the time! Check this shit out. You know Brent Hansen?"

"Who?"

"Brent Hansen! You know, fourth barracks toad. His brother is Barden Hansen, who is on the board of directors! You met him a couple of months ago at a BSA meeting!"

"Oh yeah, Brent . . . right. What about him?"

"Man, jus' now, five White boys dressed up like Klansmen went into his room and were messin' with him!"

Jon was immediately fully awake and stood straight up. He reached over and turned on his desk lamp.

"Messin' with him? How? I mean what did they do?"

"They were talking shit to him, telling him they were gonna run him out of the school. They told him he was going down. Just talking a lot of shit. Then, they burned a cross in his room on his half press!"

"What!" Jon screamed.

"Yep."

"Man, you gotta be shittin' me!"

"Uh huh."

"How do you know about all of this?"

"His roommate, Anson Weaver, came to my room after he chased them out and told me."

"His roommate chased them out. What did Brent do?"

"He froze."

"Get out of here!"

"Yep. It scared the shit out of him."

"How long ago did all of this happen?"

"Not more than thirty minutes ago."

"Where's Brent now?"

"He's in his room. He ain't doing too good. He's scared to death, still."

"Who else knows?"

"Just the five White boys, Brent, Anson, you, and me. Anson came to my room and told me what happened. Then I went with him back to his room to check on Brent. I told him not to do anything until he heard from me again."

"So, he hasn't called his brutha yet?"

"Not as far as I know. At least he hadn't yet. But you know he will soon."

"Yeah, I know. Do you have any idea who the fuck the White boys were? How many did you say there were?"

"There were five, and no I don't know who all of them were. But . . . I do know how we can find out real easy."

"How?"

"Well, when they went into the room, both Brent and Anson were sleeping. When they started talking shit to Brent and making noise, it woke Anson up. One of the guys noticed him and told him he better lie there and keep quiet if he knew what was good for him. The guy told Anson it had nothing to do with him and he'd better keep out of it or they would come back for him later. So, for a while, he just lay there. At least until they lit the cross. When they lit the cross, he jumped out of the bed. When he did, one of the White boys tried to shove him back into the bed. When he did that, Anson resisted. So, the White boy hit him. That's when all hell broke loose! Anson swung and cracked one of the White boys in the face. The impact knocked off the White boy's head dress. Anson got a good look at him and recognized him."

"What!"

"At that point, one of the White boys hit Anson in the back of the head with something.

Whatever it was, it dazed him. They rushed him, hit him a few more times, and told him that he better not tell anyone. Then they broke out the door real quick. The one whose shit got knocked off jus' picked up his stuff and ran. Anson said it all happened so fast!"

"So, he saw who it was?"

"Yep!"

"Well, who was it!" demanded Jon.

"It was Scott Myers."

"The junior?!"

"Yep."

"Well, if it was him, you know the others were juniors, too."

"Yeah, I know."

"Do you know any of the guys he hangs with?"

"A couple."

"Well, you're right, if we know him, then we got the rest of them mutha fuckas!"

"All right, so what now?"

"Well, we can't really do anything until morning. Let me think on it. I'll call you first thing in the morning. I have breakfast detail, so I'll call you right after I come back. In the meantime, don't talk to anyone about this! Don't tell anyone what has happened. We have to do this shit right. This one won't get swept under the rug. This is just what I warned the RC about! This is gonna rock this lily-white school down to its roots! Anyway, I'll talk to you later on this morning."

"All right, man."

"Adam?"

"Yeah?"

"Remember, not a word to anyone."

"You know me, 'G.'"

"Yeah, I do," Jon said sarcastically.

"Fuck you!"

"I love you too, baby. Talk to you later." Jon paused, then added, "Oh, and Adam, thanks for calling me."

"Later," Adam said with a chuckle.

Jon hung up the phone and stood motionless for a moment. He turned, walked to the window, and looked out over the parade deck. As he stood there, he slowly shook his head. After a few minutes, he walked over to his desk and turned off the lamp. Jon then climbed up into his top rack.

Jon lay in his rack staring into the dark night.

"No greater accomplice was ever created than the darkness of night," he thought aloud.

Jon sighed as he began to formulate a plan of action. He recapped the conversation he had just had with his vice president. He was still reeling with disbelief.

"Damn, this is supposed to be the 80s! This is some fucked-up shit!" he whispered.

"Ain't it though!" came the reply from the bottom rack. "But don't worry about it, room dog, I didn't hear a thing!"

In the morning, Jon returned from his breakfast detail early, picked up his phone and dialed Adam's extension.

"Hello?"

"Hey whassup, Hal? Is Adam around?"

"Yeah, Jon, he is, hold on. Oh, by the way, that was some fucked-up shit last night, wasn't it? What you guys gonna do?"

"I don't know yet, man. Hopefully, the right thing, though."

"I know you will, Jon. Awright, here's Adam."

"Before you say anything," said Adam quickly as he took the phone from his roommate. "He's my roommate and he was here last night and heard it all."

"Hey, man. I didn't say a word."

"Yeah, but I know you, mutha fucka!"

"Hey, I got a roommate too. Trust me I understand! Anyway, look, I got a plan."

"Awright, shoot."

"The first thing we do is go and get some fire power on our side. We need to go to Breck and tell him what has happened. We'll ask him what we should do. Depending on what he says, and how he's talking, we'll keep him or move on without him."

"Donald Breckenridge? Third barracks commander? Do you think we can trust him? I mean is he one of the bruthas?"

"Yeah, I do think we can trust him. Plus, I have a feeling that everyone is gonna have to pick a side. There will be no straddling the fence. Face it, man, last night the line was drawn. Now everyone has to be on one side or the other. Some of us have already made the choice. Others of us will have the choice made for us. I hope for all the Blacks' sake, they choose the right side!"

"Awright, when do we go see him?"

"Right after muster."

"Okay."

"Do you have an eight o'clock class?"

"Nope."

"Good, neither do I. I'll meet you in front of Third Barracks right after muster."

"Okay, see ya there."

As Jon approached Third Barracks, he spotted Adam talking with another Black cadet. As he drew nearer, he could hear bits and pieces of their conversation. He was relieved that the two were talking about their fraternity, not about what would become known as "the incident."

"Boy! You pretty mutha fuckas are all the same. Always talking about yourselves, primping and preening in a mirror, or dropping canes," said Jon, addressing Adam and the other cadet.

"People who live in glass houses shouldn't throw stones," Adam shot back quickly.

"Yeah, don't get us started on you and your weak-ass frat," said the other Black cadet jokingly.

"You're right, I don't want to get you started . . . No use making you burn up your few brain cells trying to create a lie."

The three cadets exchanged laughter. Soon, Adam and Jon were walking into Third Barracks and heading for Donald Breckenridge's room.

A few minutes later, the two stood at the door of the third barracks commander.

They exchanged hopeful looks.

"How's Brent?" inquired Jon.

"He's cool. I told him to let us handle it and not to worry." responded Adam.

"Do you think it'll work?"

"I guess we'll see, won't we?"

Jon let out a loud sigh and knocked loudly on the door.

"Yeah? Who is it? C'mon in," said a voice from inside the room.

Jon opened the door and walked in, followed closely by Adam.

The room was much larger than the normal cadet room, although it was not as large as the RC's room. A bed lined both the left and right walls. In the corners of the room, full presses were neatly arranged. In the front of the room sat two half presses. On the back wall, sitting under an oversized window, sat two desks. The tops had been taken off of them and were sitting at the head of each bed.

Jon was impressed with the airiness of the room. It was bright, airy, and quite neat.

Donald Breckenridge was sitting at his desk with some papers in front of him. He had obviously been signing them before Jon and Adam arrived. Donald's roommate, a White cadet, was milling around the room collecting various items, apparently for his upcoming class. Donald, looking up from signing the papers, saw the two familiar faces and smiled immediately.

"Hey guys, what's up? What brings you to the terrible third?" said Breckenridge, standing and extending his hand toward them.

"Hey Breck," said Adam, arriving at Breckenridge's hand first and shaking it.

Jon stood looking around the room as he waited for Adam to finish with his salutation. As Adam stepped to the side, Jon approached Breckenridge and shook his hand.

"Hey, Breck, what's going on?" Jon said nonchalantly.

"You guys know my roommate, Jerry Vanderbilt?"

"Hey, Jerry, how ya doin'?" said Jon.

"What's up, man," said Adam coolly.

"Hey, fellas, how ya doin'?" said Jerry Vanderbilt, pleasantly.

"Breck we need to talk to you," said Jon, seriously.

Breckenridge, sensing an unusual seriousness in Jon's nature, stepped from behind his desk and positioned himself next to the two junior cadets.

"Yeah, sure. Sit down. What is it? What's wrong?"

"Well . . .," Jon said, glancing at Breckenridge's roommate, then pausing.

"Oh, he's okay. He's cool," said Breckenridge, noticing the look on Jon's face.

Jon and Adam exchanged looks of uncertainty. Jon then looked at Breckenridge again. Breckenridge nodded his head and gave Jon a reassuring look.

"Awright, look, Breck, some real serious shit went down last night, and since you are the highest-ranking Black cadet, we're coming to you for your input."

"Yeah, I'm listening. What happened?"

"Well, I'll let Adam explain it to you, since he was the one who explained it to me."

"Well, Breck, at about 2:00 this morning . . ."

When Adam finished relaying the details of "the incident," Breckenridge and his roommate sat speechless.

"You've got to be fucking kidding," said Breckenridge finally.

"I wish we were," said Jon.

"I don't believe it!" said Jerry incredulously. "Uh, I mean I believe *you*. I can't believe something like this could happen, here."

Adam looked at Jon and rolled his eyes toward the ceiling.

"Something has got to be done! I want some ass on this one!" said Breck, visibly upset.

"You and me both," said Jon.

"Have you told anyone else about this?" asked Breck.

"No. The only ones who know are us, the involved cadets, and uh . . . all of our roommates," said Jon, turning toward Breckenridge's roommate and smiling.

"I think we need to talk to the fourth barracks commander," said Jerry.

"No, that ain't gonna be good enough," said Adam, quickly.

"You're right," agreed Breck. "We need to go to Colonel Ball."

"Exactly!" agreed Adam.

"Bingo!" said Jon.

"All right, guys, I have a nine o'clock. Let's go talk to the Colonel at ten o'clock. Is that cool for you two?"

"It's fine for me," said Adam.

"Me too," agreed Jon.

"Alright, meet me in front of Harris Hall at ten o'clock."

Jon and Adam stood up, thanked Breck and his roommate, then quickly exited the room. Silently, the two walked down the corridor, down the stairs, and out of the barracks. Once outside the barracks, they stopped and finally spoke.

"Well?" queried Adam.

"He's on board."

"Cool."

"See you at ten."

"I'll be there. Peace."

———

Jon hurried down the sidewalk in front of second barracks. As he walked, his mind was occupied with thoughts of the "incident" and how he would deal with it. He wondered how he would lead the BSA through *this* situation.

This is it, he thought. *This is the incident I warned the RC about. Now that it has happened, what will I do?*

Jon turned and headed down the street which passed in front of Long Hall.

As he walked, lost in his thoughts, someone calling out his name brought Jon out of his distraction.

"Jon! Hey, Jon!"

Jon looked up and spotted Adam standing on the next corner, waiting impatiently for him. As Jon neared Adam, Adam began talking quickly and excitedly.

"Man, you won't believe who I just saw!"

"Who?"

"Barden Hansen!"

"Get the fuck outta here!" said Jon in disbelief. "How'd he hear about it so soon?"

"I don't know, maybe he's related to one of the guys it happened to," said Adam, sarcastically. "But anyway, who cares *how* he heard? The fact is that he is here and pissed!"

"Where'd you see him?"

"He was on his way to see the Colonel. He stopped me in front of the activity center and asked me what I knew."

"What'd you tell him?"

"I told him what I knew!" Adam said with a "that's a stupid question" tone.

"Man," whispered Jon thoughtfully as he chewed on his lip.

"All right, now what?"

"Well, now we continue with our plan as if we didn't know he was here. Did he say what he was gonna do?"

"Naw, he just said, 'Somebody's gonna pay!' He was ranting and raving, though. I heard him saying something about 'Bastion of the South; Good Ole Boy; Still Living in the Slave Days, etc., etc., etc.,'"

"Whew, I bet he was fit to be tied, huh?"

"You know it! He also said he's not gonna let them get away with this. He said after he gets done talking to some people, they would have to do right by him."

"They who?"

"The M.U.T.S."

"Talk to who?"

"Man, I don't know! He wasn't exactly in the mood to be interviewed, ya know?"

"All right, nig' don't get testy! Anyway, let's get going, we have to meet Breck."

The two cadets walked down the sidewalk to the building which housed all the active duty officers, noncommissioned officers, and disciplinarian officials. It was in the lobby of this building that they were supposed to meet with Breckenridge.

After waiting almost twenty minutes, the two cadets were surprised by Barden Hansen as he walked down the lobby stairs.

"Jon! Adam!" Barden Hansen called them loudly.

The two cadets whirled around and came to attention.

"Sir?" said Jon, surprised to meet up with Barden.

"Hey Al," said Adam, unassumingly.

"What are you two doing here?"

"We came to speak with Col. Ball and get on top of this before it gets out of hand," said Jon.

"Oh?"

"Yeah, we figured he didn't know, and we'd tell him. Well, he obviously knows now, so we need to know what he is gonna do about it," Adam said.

"Hmmmmm," Barden said, looking around the lobby. He glanced upstairs to see if he saw anyone. He then motioned for the two to move closer to him.

As Jon and Adam stepped closer, Barden whispered to them. "Meet me in the library, by the research section, in ten minutes."

Jon and Adam nodded.

Barden turned and walked out of the building and got into his car, a late-model powder blue Mercedes Benz 300 CE, with tags that read "OPEN WYD." As the car started, Jon noticed the sunroof as it opened and the antenna as it slowly rose and stretched itself. Jon also noticed a cellular antenna which was positioned in the top center of the rear windshield. He watched as Barden drove off while talking on his car phone.

Jon and Adam exchanged puzzled looks, each asking the same question silently:

I wonder what he wants to talk to us about.

"So, should we go see the Colonel?" asked Adam.

"Nope. Let's meet with Al first. Plus, Breck still hasn't gotten here. Let's go, we'll worry about the Colonel and Breck later."

Ten minutes later, Jon and Adam entered the library. As they walked past the front desk, Jon noticed Barbra, one of the librarians, who sat at her desk reading a magazine. Jon stopped to talk to her as Adam continued toward the back of the library.

"Hey, sweetie," Jon said, smiling.

Recognizing the voice, Barbra looked up from her magazine and smiled.

Barbra was a very attractive woman in her early thirties. She was about 5'6", dark-skinned, with medium-length hair, beautiful white teeth, well-manicured hands, and a voluptuous hourglass body. All the Black cadets, or at least the ones who ventured into the library, tried to talk to her. She, however, only gave one of them the time of day. Jon was that one. He had been trying to get her to go out with him, but so far he had not been successful. She was either busy with her four-year-old son or Jon was busy with his . . . social life.

Barbra got up from her desk and walked over to the section of the counter where Jon was leaning.

"Whew! That dress is talking today!"

"Hey, soldier, what's new?" said Barbra, ignoring his comment.

"Us."

"Oh?"

"Yeah, this is the week you finally find time in your busy schedule for me."

"Oh, *my* busy schedule!"

"Yeah! I'm about tired of waiting for you to decide to go out with me. You know you can't keep me dangling on this rope forever. You gotta love me or leave me alone!" said Jon, feigning hurt.

"Jon you are so full of it! I don't know how you stand yourself."

"You name the time and I'll be there!"

"If I had a dollar for every time, I heard you say that!"

"Then you might be able to buy a Happy Meal! But for real, how about this weekend?"

"C'mon Jon, don't play with me."

"Seriously, how about Friday night?"

"Friday night? No, I can't do it on Friday night . . ."

"See here we go again! I knew it! Back on that string!"

"Jon, you know that's not true. It's just that I have to . . ."

"Save it," said Jon holding up his hand. "I understand. You just don't want me," Jon said sniffling.

"Okay Denzel, you can cut the act."

"No, that's fine. I have to go anyway. Maybe one day you'll see your way clear to deal with this lowly soldier who has such a crush on you," Jon said, feigning crying.

"Yeah, one day when you let loose some of your harem and you have time for me?"

"Humph! I'm insulted!" Jon said, indignantly. "Harem? What harem? I have a few young ladies who I enjoy taking a few places. When did that become a crime? If I am guilty of anything, I am guilty of loving the companionship of a Black woman. But, if I could ever get you to go out with me, I wouldn't need anyone else's companionship. If you would just let me in . . . I shudder to even think of the joy!"

"So, what about Saturday night?"

"Wooooo, would you look at the time!" Jon said tapping his wristwatch. "I'll call you, okay?"

"Just as I thought. Some people never change."

"Have you given me a good reason to?" Jon said over his shoulder as he hurried toward the back of the library.

Midway toward the back, Jon met Adam who sat patiently waiting for Jon to catch up.

"You done now?"

"Well, we can't start doing things out of the norm, it would be suspicious. We have to be careful to do things as we always have. You seen Barden?"

Adam pointed toward some bookcases in the corner of the research section. Jon peered through the spaces and saw Barden talking to his younger brother, Brent. They appeared to be arguing.

"Well," said Jon, "let's go."

Jon and Adam walked in between two bookcases and stood opposite Barden and Brent. Barden, noticing the two cadets, turned, and addressed them.

"Thank you for coming."

He then pointed to one of the aisles and motioned toward it. He and Brent went the opposite way and entered the aisle from the opposite end. The four met in the middle.

"Look, gentlemen, let me get right to the point. What happened last night was criminal, felonious, and reprehensible! Now

Brent claims he can only remember a small portion of what happened. He says he remembers them chanting racial slurs, saying they were going to run him out, making reference to him being my brother, and burning a cross. He claims he didn't recognize any of the voices. I say bullshit! He has to have an idea. Anyway, there is a good chance we will catch them because his roommate did get a look at one of them. Now, as soon as they find out who these others are, they will try to cover this whole thing up. This is where you two come in," he said pointing to Jon and Adam. "We need you to rally all the other Blacks on the yard, meet with them, and let them know what happened before they hear the amended version. We cannot let this get swept under the carpet. We just can't! We must do everything in our collective power to get as much publicity as we can out of this because, trust me, no publicity . . . no justice!"

CHAPTER 10

Jon stood at a classroom window looking at several Black cadets making their way toward the academic building he was in. There inside the classroom, several Blacks had already gathered.

Jon turned away from the window and called out to Nate.

"Nate, c'mere for a sec."

"Yeah, Jon," Nate said as he approached Jon.

"Did you give the announcement to the regimental adjutant?"

"Yep."

"Did he make the announcement?"

"Yep."

"What did it say?"

"For all Black cadets and members of the BSA to meet immediately after mess in room 128 of Baker Hall."

"Good. Thanks."

"Sure."

After about twenty minutes, the room was close to capacity. The room was alive with conversation and it did not take long for several of the cadets to start querying Jon.

"So, what's up Jon?"

"Yeah, what's this all about?"

"It must be important for you to call 'all Blacks.'"

"Did you see the look on those White boys' faces?"

"I know, they were like, 'Oh, God, they're planning a revolt!'"

"It wouldn't surprise me to see some of them show up just to see what is up."

"If they know what is good for them, they'll stay away," said Tommy.

"Yeah, well, I wanna know what's going on with this shit I heard about Brent Hansen!"

"Well, that's what this meeting is all about, so hold your horses," replied Adam.

"Look, we may as well get started," began Jon. "There are some things going on which all of you need to know about. Some real shit has gone down in the past twenty-four hours and we wanted to tell you about it. We wanted to tell you the real deal before you heard a bunch of bullshit. However, I'm gonna let Adam brief all of you on what went down last night."

Adam walked to the front of the room and began to explain the events which surrounded "the incident."

After hearing the detailed account of the events of the night before, the room was quiet for a moment.

"Now, before any of you ask questions, let me tell you that they have found out who all of the guys are. They turned themselves in. The question I pose to you is what do you think the punishment should be? They have not decided or announced anything, but if enough of us feel strongly about one particular punishment, then we'll take it to the administration. Now . . . what do you say?"

"Expel the mutha fuckas," yelled one of the cadets.

"Yeah!" agreed another.

"Naw let the fellas have 'em for thirty minutes in a room, then expel what's left of 'em," said someone from the rear of the room.

Laughter and chatter spread all over the room. Adam looked at Jon and shrugged.

"Yeah, I know. I guess we know what they want," said Jon.

"Hey! Hey!!!" Adam yelled. "So, are we in agreement? We the members of the BSA want the five White cadets, involved in last night's incident, expelled?"

"Hell, yeah," said almost every Black cadet in unison. Adam looked at Jon and they both smiled.

"I need to see the officers. As for the rest of you, we are adjourned," said Jon.

The room cleared, leaving Jon, Adam, Theo, Nate, Evan, Tim, and Tommy.

"Awright, guys, this is the deal: Adam and I spoke to Barden Hansen this afternoon. He wants us to ride this for all it's worth. I guarantee you if we let this one go, there's no telling which of us is next."

"Our next move is to go to Colonel Ball. That is purely political. It is a matter of flexing our muscles. Everyone will be looking at us to see what we will do. That's what Al was saying. If we don't flex, they'll think they can do anything. Fuck that!" concluded Adam.

"So, when do we go, and who goes?" asked Nate.

"Well, we are gonna give them the benefit of the doubt. We'll see what they do first. Then if they don't do what they're supposed to, then they'll hear from us," replied Adam.

"Any questions?" asked Jon.

The officers of the BSA shook their heads in unison.

"All right. Good. Then wait to hear from us. As soon as we know something, or as soon as it's time to move, we'll let you know. In the meantime, do not believe the lies you will undoubtedly hear," said Adam.

"Yeah, remember, if it comes from the White man and he puts it on paper, or on the air, don't believe a mutha fuckin' word of it!" interjected Tommy.

"Okay, we'll see you all soon," said Adam as he collected his cap and notepad.

After the cadets exited, Jon stepped into the hallway. One cadet, who remained after the BSA meeting was waiting for Jon and leaning causally against the wall at the end of the hall, next to the stairs.

Jon walked over to him, looked around, then whispered, "Well, it looks like you and I are gonna be getting real busy this year."

"Yeah, real busy!" said the Assassin, flashing a toothy, pearly white grin.

CHAPTER 11

It was Friday afternoon and the parade had just finished. Friday afternoons had now become one of Jon's favorite times. On Fridays after parade, he took the first several hours to just unwind and relax. Jon normally did some sort of physical activity. If it was nice outside, he played football on the parade deck. If no one were paying attention, he and the guys would sneak in a game of "rough house." If it were too cold or rainy for football, he would go to the gym and play full court basketball. Either way, he did something. Jon could not see himself just sitting idle. The very thought of sitting idle made him cringe.

On this particular Friday, as Jon was playing a game of "rough house," he heard a loud and riotous cheer come from the barracks. He heard clapping and yelling. Puzzled, Jon and the other cadets stopped and looked at each other. After a moment, they shrugged and continued to play. All the cadets continued, that is, except Jon. Jon stood looking from barracks to barracks.

"Hey, Jon, heads up!" yelled one of the cadets, referring to the ball which narrowly missed Jon's head.

Jon ducked and shot an icy glare at the one who had thrown the ball. The cadet shrugged apologetically. Out of the corner of his eye, Jon noticed someone running across the parade deck toward the area where he and the other cadets were.

"Jon! Hey, Jon!" yelled McKenzie as he approached. "You ain't gonna believe this shit!"

"What?!"

"Cuz, they just handed down the punishments," gasped McKenzie.

"Yeah?!"

"Uh huh."

Jon stared at McKenzie, waiting for his information. McKenzie, badly out of breath from his sprint across the parade deck, stood bent over with his hands on his knees.

"You really ought to stay in better shape," quipped Jon.

"I am in shape! You would be out of breath too if you sprinted from the third floor of #1 all the way out here where you all are getting high on your testosterone! Don't make me read you, Mr. Quest!" said McKenzie, straightening up and placing his hands on his hips.

"My bad, frat! Don't get touchy!"

"No, don't you get me started. I am not in the mood to lay you out!"

"Yeah, okay. Now, what about the punishments?"

"Well, they were handed down."

"And . . .?" said Jon impatiently.

"They got 120 cycles and six months' weekend isolation."

"That's it?!" Jon demanded.

"Yep."

"You've got to be kidding!"

"Uh huh."

"Fuck! So, I guess any mutha fucka can burn a cross in our rooms and dress up in white sheets and it's all right?! Naw, man, this ain't over, not by a long shot!" said Adam who had left the football game and joined in on the conversation.

"McKenzie, do me a favor and see how many of the boys you can round up. Tell them to meet me and Adam in my room in thirty minutes. Whoever you can reach, tell them to meet us right away!"

"No prob."

"Also, round up the officers of the BSA and tell them to meet us in about twenty minutes."

"Awright."

McKenzie turned and walked toward his barracks. As he departed, Jon stood motionless for a moment, then turned to the guys waiting for him on the makeshift football field.

"Can you believe that?" he asked the group.

"Ain't that some shit?" said Tyrone.

"I don't know why you jokers are surprised," snorted Adam. "Hell, these crackers ain't gonna fry their own. Had it been a brother who dressed up in all black with a black beret and gone into one of their rooms and burned a cross, or something, he'd be looking for a new college!"

"I know that's right!" agreed Tim. "They can beat you down, spit on you, dehumanize you, make you feel less than a man, castrate you, or whatever, and it's okay. But if we look at them wrong or say the wrong thing, in the wrong way, then the witch hunt begins!"

"This don't make no sense!" echoed Evan. "Bruthas have been put out o' here for much less!"

Jon was silent and still. He was staring off into the distance. He was staring at the American flag which flew from the flagpole on the east end of the parade deck. After a few minutes, Jon spoke quietly, as if to himself.

"Liberty and justice for all? The only problem is that 'All' don't include the Black man," said Jon with a disgusted grunt.

Jon then turned and faced the rest of the cadets.

"Well, Adam and I have a meeting, we'll see you all later," said Jon as he started walking towards his barracks.

After several minutes of dialogue, the group had worked itself into a frenzy.

"So, what are we gonna do now?" demanded one of the cadets.

"We are not gonna let them get away with this!" insisted Derrick.

"They have to pay!" said Tyrone.

"Yeah, and I bet you that's exactly what Adam and Jon are talking to the Assassin about right now," commented Tim. "So, at this point, all we can do is wait for the meeting we have with them and see what's up."

It was the first Tuesday of the month, the day of the regularly scheduled BSA meeting. Members of the BSA, and many curious nonmembers, had gathered in their regular meeting room and were waiting impatiently for Jon. The room was alive with energy and conversation. Everyone was abuzz about the punishment handed down to the "5" (as the white cadets would come to be known).

Adam was talking to several cadets near the front of the room. The cadets were waiting for Jon to arrive, as they were sure he would have some very interesting news for them.

Within a few minutes, Jon entered the room. As he entered, a silence fell over the entire room. He walked slowly to the end of the table and set his leather portfolio on the chair. His motions were slow and deliberate. He then squared up on the podium and looked out over the crowd.

"Whassup, y'all?" he said quietly.

"Damn, cuz, you look like you been fuckin' all night or like you ain't slept in a week! You look like shit, Jon," said Preston, one of the BSA sophomores, turning to the other members and laughing.

"Yeah? Well, I feel like I been fuckin' all night. But don't worry, yo' mama didn't get caught when I snuck her out," teased Jon.

The room erupted in laughter. Jon was glad to hear the laughter, as he believed the majority of the guys in the room would not have much to laugh about in the coming months. He himself was finding it more and more difficult to find things to laugh about. The pendulum of the mood on campus had swung noticeably. Now, the Blacks were noticeably keeping to themselves, which made the Whites that much more nervous. As Jon looked around the room, he noticed that the meeting was more crowded than usual tonight.

Why does it take tragedy for Blacks to unite? wondered Jon.

There was no doubt that life had begun to get stressful. There was also no doubt that all eyes were on him. The Black eyes were on him. The White eyes were on him. All eyes were on him.

Just the day before, the director of the college band to which Jon belonged had pulled Jon to the side and "advised" him against getting too involved in what was going on. He was sure to let Jon know that it was for his own good that he steer clear of "the incident."

No matter what happened, Jon was in a no-win situation. If he kept quiet and did not get involved, he would get along great with the Whites, but he would have sold out his position, the BSA, his race, and most importantly, himself. If he got involved, he would get along great with the BSA members and other Blacks, but life for him at the M.U.T.S. would be that much more challenging. It would be more challenging with regard to both his military and academic success. It was not a hard choice for Jon to make.

"Hey, Derrick, why don't you open us up?" said Adam.

Derrick rose and walked quickly to the podium. Jon stepped to the side and allowed him to address the audience.

"Can we all stand, bow our heads, and close our eyes? Father look down on us in our hour of need. Bless our minds and bodies. Keep us strong mentally and physically. Bless our academics and our athletics. Bless us to be wise and prudent in our decisions. And finally, Lord, bless the General to reconsider his decision and kick those five mutha fuckin' pecka woods outta here! Amen!"

"Amen!" shouted the cadets enthusiastically.

"Yeah, uh, thanks Derrick," Adam said. "Just make sure you don't sit by me. Cuz when the lightning strikes, I don't want to be too close."

"Sorry," he shrugged. "He knows the deal, though."

"Anyway," Adam laughed, "I'm not gonna prolong the time. Jon, you ready?"

"Yeah."

"Awright, at this time I yield the floor to the gentleman from Philadelphia, our Prez."

"Thanks, gentleman from Baltimore," Jon said with a smile. "Look, fellas, I'm not gonna beat around the bush. You all know what is going on. I know you all feel it. I know I do. In the up and coming weeks, things are gonna get tougher. We've got to stick together and watch one another's backs. We have got to be unified. One strong, unified voice pursuing one common goal. Now some of you in this room will sell us out or try to stay with your White friends. But, when the lines are drawn in the sand, *they* will remind you that you are Black. Then, you'll come running back to us."

Jon paused and scanned his audience to gauge the impact of his last statement. Many cadets sat expressionless. They were on the edge of their chairs, waiting to hear the full report. Other cadets looked around the room and were noticeably uncomfortable. Many of these were the ones to whom Jon had just referred.

"Now," he continued. "I have some news for all of you. The General wants to meet with the BSA."

Jon nodded his head as an affirmation to the surprised and puzzled looks.

"Why? I have no idea. But still, he does. It will be tomorrow night immediately following evening mess in the Packard Hall auditorium. I am asking, in fact I am begging, all of you to leave the mess hall immediately after second rest. I know that is a sacrifice for some of you; however, we cannot afford to have anyone coming in on CPT."

"Do we have to come?" yelled someone from the audience.

"You don't have to do anything, but live, stay Black, and die," Jon responded. "However, we need to do the politically correct thing. So, everyone needs to be there. All of you are always talking shit about saying this or that to the General. Well, now's it's all of our chances. I am sure we won't get another. So even if it kills you, please be there. It won't be good enough for me to continue to talk to the General or the colonel. They have to know that I am echoing the sentiments of the organization. There is strength in numbers. We have to show them it is not just me and Adam who are pissed off. That's all I want to cover today. We'll see you tomorrow. Thanks for coming."

Jon stepped away from the podium, took a seat at the table, and began to look through some papers. There was immediate noise and conversation as the cadets rose and collected their belongings. Some of the cadets wondered aloud about why the General could possibly want to meet with the BSA. Others answered the question aloud, asserting that he merely wanted to pat them on the head, tell them everything would be okay, and send them shuffling on their way.

Jon had no idea what the General wanted, either. However, the one thing he did know was that it promised to be an interesting meeting.

CHAPTER 12

Adam stood on the platform at the front of the theater-style auditorium. Jon sat at a table which was positioned to the right of Adam. Adam stared at the door for a while, then consulted his watch. He shook his head in disgust as three cadets hurried into the room. Adam looked at Jon and rolled his eyes toward the ceiling.

Once again, Adam looked at the door and at JT. JT stood at the door with one large hand resting on the door handle and the other held in front of his face, so he could see his watch and Adam without moving his head.

As Adam watched the door, seven cadets entered noisily.

"Ay, hurry up and find a seat!" commanded Adam.

JT looked at Adam reassuringly and gave him the thumbs-up. Adam nodded his head with a sigh. He then looked at Jon and gave him the thumbs-up. Jon smiled, stood up, and faced the BSA members.

"Thanks," he said to Adam.

Jon held his arm up and turned his watch toward the BSA members.

"It's time," he whispered loudly.

In the rear of the room, JT snapped to attention. "Room, atten-chun!" he yelled loudly.

The entire room jumped to their feet and snapped to attention. The General, and his entourage, which included the commandant of cadets, the assistant commandant of cadets, the college executive officer, and the director of public relations for the college, entered the room and proceeded down the aisle to the stage area. While the others took their seats, the General centered himself among the cadets and began to speak.

"You may be seated. I would like to thank you for coming this evening. I would also like to thank cadets Quest and Terreaux for arranging this meeting. The reason I wanted to talk to you is because of the recent events. I want to let you know that we have every intention of ensuring this kind of thing does not continue. However, I need all of you to help me with something also. We have gotten complaints of racial harassment and intimidation, which are erroneous. For instance, one Black cadet reported a cadet was wearing a sheet and a pointed head piece and was shouting racial threats and slurs from a third-story barracks window. We investigated and found a cadet who had a ceremonial headpiece which was pointed, and it was hanging in a window with a light-colored outfit. So, you see, this report was incorrect. You cannot let your imaginations get the best of you. Do not worry about the five cadets; they have been severely punished and will serve their punishment in full. The system has dealt with them. It is not in order for any of you to deal with them. One of the five cadets has been severely beaten. He claims he slipped in the shower; however, we have some witnesses who say they saw a group of Black cadets dressed in black enter and exit his room on the night he was beaten. We cannot and will not tolerate such behavior! Before you go gathering vigilante groups together, you should know the real story. This whole incident was seriously blown out of proportion. The facts of the case were overlooked in the emotionalism of it all. The five cadets did not burn a cross in the room, as it has been said. The cross had already been burned by the time they came into the room. They did not burst into the room yelling racial slurs. They all filed in quietly and whispered things like 'We're gonna run you out'; 'You're too slack'; 'You don't belong here'; 'You're only here because of your brother.' See? That is not racial. Heck, if it had not been for the ridiculous hats, this would not have been racial. Gentlemen, this is the eighties. We need to stop wearing our feelings on our sleeves. We are not Black or White, here at the Military University. Here, we are all gray. This is the long gray line, not the long white or black line. Let us not blow this any further out of proportion. Oh, and let us all remember what the rule book says about talking to outside agencies regarding college information."

The General looked around the room and mustered a phony, wry smile. He looked over at his entourage and nodded. They rose and the commandant turned to JT and nodded. By now, the General was halfway up the aisle, headed toward the door.

JT rose to his feet and yelled, "Room, atten-chun!"

The cadets half-heartedly stood to their feet.

"Excuse me, General!" said Jon, loudly. "I am sure there are several questions which our members would like to ask you."

The General stopped dead in his tracks. He paused a moment, then turned and glared at Jon, coldly.

"General, I am sure you had every intention of listening to us, as we did you, as well as entertaining any questions we may have had," said Adam, pointedly.

"The General is a remarkably busy man. He is on a tight time schedule," volunteered the commandant.

"We are well aware of that," snapped Jon. "Therefore, the sooner he starts answering our questions, the sooner he will be able to accommodate his busy schedule. Whoever planned his schedule should be advised that it is always in good taste to plan a Q&A period after any address to a group. Isn't that so, General?" said Jon.

"Yes, uh, yes, of course, Mr. Quest. I would, uh, be happy to field a few questions. We just did not think that, uh, there would be any, uh, any questions," stammered the General as he returned to the front of the room.

"Thank you, Sir. I am sure you will find out that with our group, there are always questions."

Jon stepped up on the platform and addressed the group.

"Gentlemen, please be seated. I am sure all of you have a million questions for the General, however, we don't have that much time. We have . . ." Jon turned and looked at the General, then at the commandant. Both stared at him icily. ". . . okay, we have 15 minutes, max! When you ask your question, please rise, and address the General. I do not need to remind you that he is the president of our college, a three-star General, a highly decorated man, a veteran of an American war, and truly deserving of all of our honor and respect," said Jon with a hint of sarcasm. "Now, who goes first?"

Several cadets were immediately on their feet. Jon looked around at the cadets standing stone-faced and erect.

"All right, everyone standing will ask one question and then be seated. We will only take questions from those now standing. To be fair, we will start from left to right. Okay Tony, you're first."

"Thank you. Good evening, General Helmsley, Sir. Cadet Lieutenant Weaver, 'A' Company athletic officer. Sir, how do you consider this being blown out of proportion, considering the attire of the five, its racial implications, and the cross, Sir?"

"Well, son, whether we admit it or not, this is college and the boys here are only eighteen, nineteen, twenty, or twenty-one. I mean, boys will be boys. They were just having fun. It was definitely in poor taste and bad judgment, but still it was boyish fun."

A collective mumble went around the room.

"Gentlemen, please," said Jon, holding his hand up. "Okay, Chris."

"Cadet Squad Sergeant DeSaussure, Tango Company, Sir. General, how do you justify the light punishment the five were given, Sir?"

"Well, young man, their punishment is by no means light. If you were to look at the PLs since the school started, you would see that their punishment is the stiffest in the history of the University. The stiffest, that is, short of expulsion. By the way, young man, that was an amazing hit you put on that receiver last week. It was that turnover which helped us win the game!"

"Thank you, Sir," said Cadet DeSaussure

"Moving right along," said Jon. "Tim, you're next."

"Cadet Corporal Burton, 'F' Troop, Sir. General Helmsley, Sir, speaking of expulsion, why didn't they get expelled? I mean, what they did was pretty serious. What does it take to get expelled, Sir?"

"We reviewed the entire case based on its facts and did not feel the deed warranted expulsion. My God, they were just having fun! They were just playing a joke. It was a college prank for Christ's sake!" said the General, his volume increasing as he became visibly irritated.

"Thank you, General. Sir, we only have two more questions for you. Gerry," said Jon.

"Cadet Senior Private Blade, Lima Company. General, how many other racial incidents have been reported this year?"

"Well," the General said slowly, "we have had two others, to my knowledge.

However, we investigated both of them and found they were not racial in intent. They were either overreactions or misunderstandings."

"Okay, the last question, Owen," said Jon.

"Cadet Platoon Sergeant Parry, 'F' Troop, Sir. General Helmsley, Sir, how soon will the cadets start serving their punishment and how do we know they won't receive a reprieve?"

"Well, to answer your first question," said the General, "the PL comes out on Monday mornings. So, their punishment starts not this week, but next. As far as your second question, I believe a 'no reprieve, no cut, no cancel' clause was attached to their Punishment Orders."

"Thanks, Owen," said Jon. "General, you will check to be sure about the clause, won't you? And if there is no such clause, we have your word one will be added, don't we, Sir?"

The General cleared his throat and looked at the commandant. The commandant stood there with a "don't look at me" look on his face.

"Uh, yes, Mr. Quest, you have my word," said the General.

"Thank you, Sir. We, the Black Students Association, appreciate you taking the time to meet and talk with us. Oh, and Sir," Jon said, turning and looking directly at the General, "for the record, Sir, we don't consider racial intimidation and racially motivated threats as college fun and games. We don't joke like that. It is far too offensive and dangerous. And with regard to the cadet who unfortunately slipped in the shower, the BSA does not have anything to do with any vigilante groups and does not support any such group in any fashion."

Upon completion of his sentence, Jon whirled around to JT and nodded.

"Room, atten–chun!" yelled JT.

The General stared at Jon for a moment. His stare was one of intense hatred. After a moment, the General moved quickly toward the door, followed closely by his entourage. A minute later, they were all gone, and the room was quiet.

"All right, seats!" yelled JT.

Suddenly, the room was alive with conversation. Conversations all over the room were the same. The cadets were collectively insulted, upset, and astonished. They could not believe the things the General had said.

"Whew!" said Adam as he stepped up on the platform. "What do ya think of that BS?!"

"Man, I bet they weren't gonna give them anything!" said one of the cadets in the group.

"If it had o' been anyone other than Brent, they woulda got off scot-free," said another cadet.

"I feel as though they shoulda gotten kicked out, fuck the dumb shit!" said yet another cadet.

"Jon, what was he talking about in the rule book?" asked one of the cadets.

"Well, there is a paragraph in the rule book which forbids the revealing of college information, 'goings-on,' etc., to the media or any other group outside the college," Jon stated. "It's too late for that, though," said Adam, shooting a grin at Jon.

Jon, noticing the grin, winked at Adam. "Well, guys, there it is. Right from the ass's, I mean, the donkey's, I mean the horse's mouth," Jon said, fighting back a smile. "You all can go. If you have any news, or hear of any, call me or Adam, immediately. Now, go study."

"Wait, Jon," yelled one of the cadets. "I want to know more about this cadet who 'slipped in the shower.' What's up with that? Do we know who did it?"

"Trust me, what you don't know *could* hurt you! Now . . . go study!"

Jon, who was standing on the platform talking with other members of the BSA, looked around and addressed the cadets on the platform.

"They have done what they're gonna do . . . now we gotta do what we gotta do. A lot of talk is not necessary. It is even dangerous. If we let this pass, it will happen again and again. If not to someone else, then to you. If not to you, then to someone else. If not to any of us, then to someone coming behind us. We ain't leavin' that kind of legacy. We ain't goin out like that!" Jon exclaimed. "Now it is time for us to unleash our dogs!"

Jon caught the eye of the Assassin, who nodded, knowingly.

The cadets on the platform exchanged serious looks, shook hands, and then exited the room.

CHAPTER 13

The phone in Jon's room rang. It was 3:30 in the afternoon and Jon was sitting at his desk working on homework from his constitutional law class. The ring signaled to Jon that the call was from off campus. The phone rang again, and Jon tentatively picked up the handset.

"Hello," said Jon.

"Uh, hello, may I speak to, uh, Jonny Quest?" said an unfamiliar voice on the other end of the phone.

"Who's calling?" inquired Jon, suspiciously.

"My name is Paul Meary. I'm from the *Star Ledger.*"

"Hello, Paul, this is Jon. What can I do for you?" said Jon with a sigh of relief.

"Well, Jonny, uh, do you prefer Jon or Jonny?"

"Jonny is fine."

"Okay. Well, Jonny, I heard you are the president of the Black students group at your college. I wanted to ask your opinion of the recent events and the punishment the five White cadets received."

"All right, so ask," Jon said dryly.

"Well, what do you think about the administration and the punishment they handed down?"

123

"Look, Paul, whatever your name is, I don't know how you got my number, but I have no interest in talking to any paper about anything. I don't talk to just any old reporter who calls here looking for a story. I would appreciate it if you would lose my number and not call me again. Now, if you don't mind, I have college to complete. Oh . . . by the way, the punishment is a joke. It is unacceptable and insulting. It shows exactly what the administration thinks about its Black cadet student body. In short, it sucks!" said Jon as he slammed the handset down.

Jon was incensed. He knew the call was a trap, yet he could not help but to add the final comments. He knew his comments would make their way back to the Administration.

"Who the fuck was that?" asked Tyrone.

"Some reporter. He wanted to ask me some questions about 'the incident.'"

"How'd he get your number?"

"I don't know, and I really don't give a shit. Anyway, you're my witness, you heard what I told him."

"Yeah," chuckled Tyrone. "So, did he . . . loud and clear."

Jon smiled and turned again to his homework.

Jon sat at the desk in his room, writing a letter to his girl-friend. It had been two days since his "chat" with the reporter from the *Star Ledger*. However, the conversation still bothered him. Something wasn't right. Something did not feel right. How did the guy get his number? How did someone from the outside know he was the president of the BSA? Who gave him this information? How did he know about Jon in the first place? As Jon sat deep in thought, his phone rang. The ring startled Jon. The second ring indicated to Jon that the call was an on-campus call.

Probably Adam, he thought to himself.

"Yeah, what up?"

"Mr. Quest?" said the female voice on the other end of the phone.

"Yeah? I mean yes ma'am," Jon said as he tried to place the voice.

"Mr. Quest, Colonel Benjamin would like to see you in his office immediately."

"Uh, yes ma'am. I'll be right there."

Jon pressed the switch hook on his phone and dialed Adam's number.

"What up?" answered Adam, casually.

"Yo, man, guess what."

"Ummm, let me guess . . . we just elected the first brutha to the White House."

"Naw, man . . . you know that will never happen!"

"Then we must have just elected the first sistah as the Vice President."

"Ha! C'mon man, for real."

"I don't know. If it ain't any of that, ain't shit else important."

"Seriously, man. Check this out: Colonel Benjamin's office just called, and he wants to see me immediately."

"Word?"

"Yup."

"What for?"

"Hell if I know."

"Damn! What does the director of Public Relations want with yo' black ass?"

"I betcha it has something to do with that reporter who called me a couple days ago."

"Oh snap! Yeah!"

"I told you something was up with that. Yo' man, we gotta be careful. The war has begun. Watch your back. I'm out."

"Good luck. Peace." Jon hung up the phone and grabbed his jacket and cap. As he ran out of his door, he passed Tyrone.

"Back in a bit. Don't wait up for me, hon," Jon said with a grin.

Jon walked into Colonel Benjamin's office and up to the secretary's desk. "Excuse me, ma'am. I'm Cadet Quest, here to see the colonel, at his request."

"Yes, Mr. Quest, he is waiting for you."

The secretary picked up the handset of the phone and pressed a button. "Sir, Cadet Quest has arrived . . . Yes, sir."

The secretary hung up the phone and looked up at Jon. "He'll be right out," she informed Jon.

Seconds later, Colonel Benjamin emerged through his doorway. He was armed with his phony public relations smile and an ersatz warmth. To Jon's surprise, he was followed by Colonel Goodman, the assistant to the president of the University.

"Mr. Quest! How are you today? C'mon in!" said Colonel Benjamin, motioning with his hand toward his office.

Jon looked at Colonel Goodman, who then smiled at him. "Good afternoon, Mr. Quest."

"Good afternoon, Sir," said Jon, attempting to cloak his surprise.

Jon marched into Colonel Benjamin's office and positioned himself in front of the huge redwood desk and assumed the position of attention.

"At ease, at ease," said Colonel Benjamin. "Relax, Mr. Quest. Colonel Goodman and I just want to talk to you for a minute."

"Mr. Quest, I'm sure no one has to tell you how the sensitivity of this, uh, 'incident,' dictates special treatment with regard to outsiders and the media. We, here on the inside, understand our system. But outsiders don't. And they would like nothing better than to smear and deface the University's impeccable name and reputation. Mr. Quest, a lot of very influential and powerful people would be very upset with anyone who would assist with such actions. Do I make myself clear?" said Colonel Goodman.

"Crystal clear, Sir," said Jon, still somewhat confused.

"In other words, Mr. Quest, alumni would not look very favorably on anyone who would leak negative information about the University to the press," said Colonel Benjamin.

"Now, Mr. Quest," said Colonel Goodman. "We are aware that you have initiated contact with the press—"

"No, Sir, I haven't," Jon interrupted.

"Son, remember the Honor Code from the Gold Book," said Colonel Benjamin.

"Sir, I do remember my Honor Code, and I haven't initiated contact with the press," Jon said.

"Then where did this come from?" asked Colonel Goodman, thrusting the prior day's edition of the *Star Ledger* toward Jon.

"Sir?" said Jon, surprised and confused.

"It says in here that you contacted them and volunteered to give them a story. The reporter said you were quite agreeable and encouraged him to ask more questions."

The two colonels, one standing beside the desk and the other standing behind the desk, stared hard at Jon.

"Sirs, first of all, I don't know how the reporter got my number. I didn't call him, he called me. Second, I told him I wasn't going to talk to any newspaper, and then I hung up on him. My roommate can corroborate that story."

"Was that before or after you told him you didn't agree with the administration's handling of the punishment and that the administration sucks?!"

"Sir, I didn't say that the administration sucks. What I said was that the punishment sucks."

"I thought you didn't talk to the reporter?!"

"No, Sir, I merely commented as I hung up that—"

"Oh, come clean, Mr. Quest! You know you talked to the reporter!"

"No Sir! I—"

"Look, Mr. Quest," said Colonel Benjamin, "I think we can all learn a valuable lesson from this. The press is tricky. That is why we don't want you cadets dealing with them. That's my job. I know how to deal with them. They'll eat you alive. So, use this as a learning experience. We'll forget this ever happened as long as you remember the Gold book rules. Whenever you are contacted by the press, just say no. Tell them they'll have to call me. That will free you up to do what you came here to do, and that is to graduate. It would be a shame if you got all tied up and preoccupied with this and did not graduate. You do want to graduate . . . don't you, Mr. Quest?"

"Yes, Sir," said Jon quietly as he noticed the strange look on the colonel's face. He definitely caught the hidden meaning in that message.

"You understand our position and I'm sure you'll do everything in your power to cooperate from here on out, won't you, Mr. Quest?" said Colonel Benjamin as he pasted on a cosmetic smile while patting Jon on the shoulder.

"Yes, Sir," said Jon, moving out of the colonel's reach.

"See, Goody, I told you Mr. Quest was a smart boy," said Colonel Benjamin to Colonel Goodman with a trace of brazenness.

"Mr. Quest, you're dismissed. Just remember our little talk today. We'll see you at your graduation."

"Yes, Sir."

Jon saluted, did an about face, and quickly exited the office. Once in the hallway, Jon looked over his shoulder and saw the two colonels watching him as he walked down the corridor. They stood stone-faced and serious as they whispered to each another.

Jon walked through the double French doors which led to the executive corridor. Once through the doors, he turned left and headed down the long hall. After a few feet, he looked behind him only to see an empty hallway. Stopping, he let out a loud sigh.

"Whew! Goddam! I can't believe that!" said Jon aloud. He leaned the back of his head against the hallway wall and rubbed his face with both hands. He remained there for a moment, collecting his thoughts. Upon hearing voices, he continued down the hall and out of the building.

"Man, I need a drink," he whispered to himself.

Jon and Tyrone sat in their room, at their respective desks, laughing. Tyrone was relaying a story about life in D.C.

". . . so anyway, I would pull up to the old lady and ask her if she needed a ride. Then I would whip out the business card. Bam!" Tyrone said, pulling out an imaginary card and putting it inches from Jon's face. "The card said, 'Brown Cab.' So, they would get in. I would load their stuff into the trunk and drive them all over the place before I took them to where they wanted to go. Man, they would have a ball and boy would I get paid!"

"Man, that is so wrong to take advantage of the elderly like that!" laughed Jon.

"Take advantage! Man puh-leez! I would talk to them and they loved it. They enjoyed the company and the attention. They also enjoyed getting out of their houses. They imparted some serious wisdom on me too.

"Man, you are such an opportunist!"

"And you know that!" said Tyrone, then picked up a pencil and flicked it at Jon. Jon ducked away from the flying pencil then got up, walked over to the racks and climbed up on his top rack. He rolled over on his back and interlocked his fingers behind his head.

"Man, I am so tired," Jon said.

"I don't know why. Every night you're out like a light when you hit the rack."

"Yeah, until I hear the door open."

"I know that's real! Man, I believe I could be in a coma and still hear that doorknob turn."

"But you want to know what's real?"

"What's that?"

"I'll tell you what's real. Ever since we started keeping those clubs under our pillows, that doorknob don't turn as much. That's what's real!"

"Hello!"

"Hey, man, what is the deal with Brown? Did those guys really make him tell those jokes at mess today?"

"Yep."

"Why didn't he refuse?"

"Supposedly he did. Then they threatened him. They told him they would drag his black ass out of the rack and make him wish he would have told the jokes."

"Get outta here! Who did it? Do you know?"

"Of course, I know."

"Oh, excuse me, I forgot who I was talking to. Man, we ought to catch those guys out somewhere and fuck them up! I wish I knew who it was. What barracks are they in?"

"Four."

"Can the Assassin get to them there?"

"Yep."

"Call and tell him. He'll go down and 'talk" to them for you."

"Nope."

"Nope?! Why not? You got a better idea?"

"Yep."

"What? What!?"

"Tyrone, I am trying to rest, damn! Look man, I've got it under control. Now we'll just have to wait to see what happens."

"See what happens?! I'll tell you what will happen . . . nuthin'! Not a goddam thing! Damn man, when are we gonna learn that those White mutha fuckas don't give a shit about us! When you gonna learn that reporting it to the administration don't mean shit!"

"Thank you for your thought-provoking and heartfelt editorial, Tyrone. Now if you don't mind, I would like to get some rest."

"Fuck it, I'm gonna go take a shower," said Tyrone angrily.

"By the way," Jon said quietly, "I said I've got it under control. I didn't say anything about reporting it to administration. You said that. I said we'll just have to wait to see what happens."

Tyrone, who was putting on a shower robe, stopped and whirled around to look at Jon.

"So, what are you gonna do?!"

There was no answer from his roommate. The only answer came a moment later when Jon let out a snore. Knowing what that meant, Tyrone waved him off with a disgusted sigh, grabbed his towel, and headed out of the door to the showers. The door slammed behind him as he left.

Jon lay motionless for a moment. After making sure Tyrone was gone, he opened his eyes, lifted up his head, and looked around the empty room. He threw his legs over the side of his rack, jumped down, walked over to the phone, picked up the receiver, and dialed a number he now regularly dialed. After two rings, a voice came on the line.

"Yeah?"

"Whassup, it's me."

"Yeah, you need work put in?"

"Howard, room 4327; Stephens, room 4102; Bradbury and Henderson, room 4418; McLaughlin, room 4239; lesson one."

"Done."

Jon hung up the phone and smiled. "Under control," he said aloud.

CHAPTER 14

It was Tuesday evening and Jon was at the regular BSA meeting. Adam was talking to the group about the dangers of dealing with reporters. "I know you all heard how they tried to set Jon up," said Adam.

The cadets in the room all nodded as they looked over at Jon.

"Well, you can never be too careful. As a matter of a fact, the best thing to do is let me and Jon deal with the media. No one talks to the media but me and Jon. Anyone got a problem with that?" Adam looked around the room daring anyone to object. "Good. Now that's all I have. I am gonna turn the rest of the meeting over to Jon."

Jon rose and approached the podium. "Thanks, 'A.T.,'" Jon said, patting Adam on his shoulder as they passed each other. "Awright, fellas, I want to discuss something very serious tonight. It has to do with the singing and playing of 'Dixie.' How many of you freshmen sing 'Dixie' when they tell you to?"

Several of the Black freshmen sheepishly raised their hands.

"Don't be ashamed. I will assume it is pure ignorance or fear which allows you to sing. Either way, from this point forward, don't! If they try to make you, take the push-ups instead. Don't be afraid of them getting mad. There is only so much they can do. If they overstep their authority, tell us and we'll take care of them." Jon shot a quick glance at the Assassin, who nodded. "Now, during the games, regardless of whether it is football or basketball, when they start singing or playing 'Dixie,' all Blacks are to sit down, with mouths closed! No one can make you do anything. This will be our way of silently protesting the way we get treated, even though it is us running or dribbling the ball."

"What about the band members, Jon?" came a question from the group.

"Well, as you well know, I am in the band. So, what I am going to tell you to do, I will take the immediate flack for. But that's cool. When they get ready to play 'Dixie,' or tell you to get ready, do not bring your instruments up to your mouths. Remain at the attention, with your instrument at your side."

"Isn't that asking for trouble, though?"

"Wasn't dressing like Klansmen and going into one of our rooms? Wasn't insulting our intelligence by calling it a joke? Wasn't saying we blew it out of proportion? You damn right it was, and you damn right it is! But see, White people don't understand anything except force, power, and rebellion. We ain't gonna get shit if we keep steppin' and fetchin'. We got to let them know we don't play that shit. We got to let them know we ain't happy and we ain't gonna just go away!"

The room was silent for a moment. Jon looked around at the faces of his BSA members. Several of the members nodded in agreement. Some seemed deep in thought, and a few looked as if they had seen a ghost.

"Look guys, nuthin' comes easy. We didn't start this. But if we don't take part in it and let our voices be heard, we may as well go back home. Because should we ignore this, we won't be able to stay because they'll run all of us out of here."

"I don't know what you guys are so worried about anyway," interjected Adam. "If someone says something, just tell them Jon and Adam told you to or not to do it. That's as good as they want it anyway."

Suddenly, everyone was nodding in agreement.

The campus was buzzing as it normally did on Fridays. Fridays were Parade Days.

Jon stood in his room looking out of his first-floor window at the parade deck. The grounds crew was busy preparing for the regular Friday afternoon parade; the whole campus was alive. Cadets ran past the window on their way to play basketball, or lift weights, or jog. Meanwhile, Tyrone sat polishing his parade gear. As Jon stared outside, deep in thought, the phone rang.

"Yeah?" said Tyrone as he grabbed the phone on the second ring. There was a pause, then Tyrone turned to Jon. "Yo, it's for you."

"Who is it?" Jon asked without turning around.

"Colonel Henderson's secretary."

"Oh?" said Jon as he turned and reached for the phone. "Hello."

"Mr. Quest?" said the female voice on the other end of the phone.

"Yes, ma'am."

"Colonel Henderson would like to see you in his office immediately."

"Yes, ma'am. I'll be right over." Jon hung the phone up and exchanged curious looks with Tyrone.

"What reporter you been talkin' to now?" said Tyrone playfully.

"Ain't no tellin'. Man, you know me."

"Be back for parade?"

"Dunno. Should be though. If I'm not, go ahead and start without me," Jon said with a grin. Jon picked up his cap and headed out the door to Colonel Henderson's office.

Several minutes later, Jon was seated on the oak bench outside Colonel Henderson's office. As he waited to be called in, he wondered what the commandant of cadets could possibly want with him. It had been a while since anything had happened. He hadn't had any late-night visitors. It was pretty much quiet, as far as he knew.

"Mr. Quest! C'mon in," said Colonel Henderson, who was standing in his doorway smiling from ear to ear.

"Yes, Sir," Jon said, standing and snapping to attention.

Colonel Henderson walked over and sat behind his desk. Jon walked into the office and up to Colonel Henderson's desk. Standing two feet in front of the desk, he stopped and executed a salute.

"Sir! Cadet Quest reporting as ordered, Sir!"

"Sit down, Mr. Quest," said Col. Henderson as he returned the salute from his seat behind the desk.

"Yes, Sir."

Jon sat down on the edge of the nearest chair. He placed his cap in his lap, sat up erect, and looked at the colonel. The colonel, who was leaning back in his chair, was studying Jon. Jon sat looking at the colonel, daring not to speak. It seemed as if they sat there for half an hour. Finally, Jon broke the silence.

"Sir, you wanted to see me about something?"

"Yes, yes, I did. Tell me, Mr. Quest, what makes you tick?"

"Excuse me, Sir?" said Jon, perplexed.

"What makes you tick? What motivates you? I'm an old Army man myself. My job was to motivate or separate. If I couldn't motivate 'em, I sure as hell could separate 'em."

"Well, Sir . . .," Jon said hesitantly.

"I mean I've heard all about what you've done as the Black Students Association President." The colonel fingered through several stacks of papers on his desk.

"Um. Uh huh. Uh huh."

The colonel looked up at Jon.

"You initiated an adoption program at an area orphanage. You started a cadet tutoring program at one of the local high schools. You started a role model program with several state high schools. You initiated a program to sponsor a child in Africa. You have taken the organization out of a $7,000 hole. You have run a very successful PR campaign with religious and civic leaders. You achieved cadre both your sophomore and junior years. You were company clerk and now are a platoon sergeant. You have never been on the PL. You are on the football, cross-country, and track teams. You are in the concert, marching, pep, and jazz bands. You have a loyal following that would do anything you tell them. I could go on and on." Colonel Henderson looked over the top of his glasses at Jon. "Impressive. Very impressive. So . . . what makes you tick?"

"Well, Sir . . .," Jon began.

"You are very powerful and influential, both on and off campus. Abuse of such power could be detrimental. Don't you agree?"

"Yes, Sir, I do and that's why—"

"Yes, yes. Hmmm. . .," said Colonel Henderson, again cutting Jon off. "Tell me, Mr. Quest, would you ever use your power and influence to hurt this institution?"

"No, Sir," Jon said half-heartedly.

"Mr. Quest, you and I can work together. Together we can achieve your goals. Let's face it . . . you need me, and I need you. However, this will not work if you go running around here like some damned cult leader making your boys rebel against the system!" said Colonel Henderson, banging his fist on the top of his desk.

"I'm sorry, Sir," said Jon, feigning ignorance, "I am not sure I understand what you are talking about."

"We heard that you told all your boys not to sing 'Dixie' and to sit down when it is played at the games. We cannot tolerate such rebellion against the system."

"Sir, first of all, 'Dixie' is not a part of the system. Second, because our conscience will not permit us to play or sing 'Dixie,' that does not constitute rebellion!"

"Your conscious, hell! The thing that is stopping your boys from singing and playing 'Dixie' is you and Mr. Terreaux!"

"Sir, they are not boys, and neither am I. I would appreciate it if you would not call us that."

Colonel Henderson glared at Jon. "Mr. Quest, is it true you have been talking to reporters?" Colonel Henderson asked calmly.

"Yes, Sir, it is," Jon shot back, coolly.

"You are aware of Section 3, Paragraph 4 of the Cadet Code of Conduct in the Gold Book, aren't you?"

"Yes, Sir, I am."

"Then you must realize you are in violation of that section. We have been overlooking it in the past. However, I can see to it that our rules are followed and enforced."

"Sir, Section 3, Paragraph 4 of the Gold Book prohibits any cadet from divulging any school information to the media. However, Sir, it does not prohibit a cadet from talking to the media and giving his opinion on issues which pertain to the world in which we live. Therefore, Sir, though I am aware that you can have the rules followed and enforced, they would not apply to anything I have said or done."

Colonel Henderson turned red and clinched his teeth. "Mr. Quest, you are dismissed."

Jon leaped to his feet, centered himself on the colonel's desk, and saluted.

The colonel waved him out.

Jon did a perfect "about face" and headed for the door.

"Oh, Mr. Quest . . ."

Jon stopped and turned around. "Yes, Sir?"

"You are excused from parade today."

"Sir?"

"I said you are excused from parade today. You do not have to go. Stay in your room. Get some rest."

"Yes, Sir." Jon exited the colonel's office wondering why the colonel had excused him from parade. He had plenty of time to get dressed and ready. When Jon got back to his room, his roommate was gone. Jon took off his clothes and climbed onto the top rack. He heard the voices, the band warming up, cadets scurrying around preparing for parade.

Jon thought about Mr. Simon. He had not talked to Mr. Simon much since his freshman year. Though he liked Mr. Simon and appreciated his wisdom, Jon felt guilty talking to him. Jon felt like he was betraying Jon Sr.'s advice and direction.

I have to handle this shit myself, Jon often thought to himself, though from time to time he privately wished he could cry on someone's shoulder. But Jon knew he had to figure this out himself. He knew he had to be a man. Man up. Handle his business. He was sure he could figure this out. He just needed uninterrupted time to focus. He needed to take time and just think all this through. He needed to lay there and develop a plan, a strategy. But he was tired. So tired. Somewhere after that, he drifted off to sleep.

CHAPTER 15

J on woke up with a jump as he heard someone yelling his
name. The voice was getting closer and closer. Suddenly the
door flew open and in walked Jamie O'Halloran. Jon quickly sat
up in his bed and tried to wipe the sleep out of his eyes.

Jamie O'Halloran was in the bagpipe section of the band
and was the head piper. He was a big red-haired Irish man. He
was about 6'2", 220 lb. He was stocky and muscular. O'Halloran
was a senior and he and Jon had never been particularly friendly.
O'Halloran had never said anything to Jon and Jon had never
said anything to O'Halloran.

O'Halloran, standing in the middle of Jon's room, was beet
red. He was huffing and puffing as if he had just run several
miles. "Why did you do it?" he demanded.

"Do what, Jamie?" Jon asked, still groggy.

"You know what I'm talking about, boy!" snarled Jamie.

"No, I don't, and I got you and yo' mama's boy swingin'!"

O'Halloran stepped closer to Jon and pointed a finger in his
face. "You told all the Black guys not to play 'Dixie'!"

"Says who?!"

"I know you did. They wouldn't have all done it by themselves, at the same time!" O'Halloran yelled.

"Yeah, so what's that got to do with me?" said Jon coolly.

KEN GORDON

"You did it. You did it and I know you did. They didn't even bring their instruments up to their mouths for Christ's sakes!"

"Get out of my room, O'Halloran," Jon said casually.

"I'm gonna tell you this, boy. If they ever do that again, I'm holding you responsible." Suddenly, O'Halloran grabbed Jon by the scruff of the collar. "And if it does happen again, I'm gonna bounce you off a couple walls."

Jon, remaining calm and still, had one hand on the club he kept under his pillow.

"O'Halloran, if you don't get your got-damn hands off me, you'll wish you had."

"Oooooo, I'm shivering." O'Halloran shoved Jon back as he released him.

Jon looked at O'Halloran for a moment then began to laugh.

"What's so funny?" asked O'Halloran.

"You just fucked up real bad," laughed Jon.

O'Halloran gave him a puzzled look for a moment, then turned to leave the room.

"You just remember what I said, boy. If it happens again . . ."

"Jamie . . ."

O'Halloran, halfway out the door, stopped and turned around.

"There is nothing that you or anyone else can do to or about me. Your threats are empty. But don't worry about that. You put your hands on me and threatened me. That I won't forgive. You fucked up, boy! Now go back to your room and think about that."

"Screw you," yelled O'Halloran!

Jon's door slammed shut. Jon got out of his bed, walked to his door, and cracked it. Outside he saw cadets milling around. Across the barracks, he saw Jamie O'Halloran go into his room and slam the door. Jon walked over to his telephone, picked up the receiver, and dialed a familiar number. The phone rang twice, and a voice came on the other end.

"Hey man, it's me."

"Whassup, you got work you need me to put in?"

"Room 2137 . . . right now!"

"Cool."

Jon hung up the phone and waited. In the distance, he heard a boom box blasting rap music. The sound grew louder and louder. Jon sat at his desk as the sound began echoing, meaning the boom box was being carried through the front entrance of his barracks. Jon walked over to his door and opened it. Outside he saw the back of Tommy, boom box on his shoulder, as he walked toward Room 2137.

Tommy played defensive end for the football team. He was 6' 5 ½" and weighed about 270 lb. Tommy was one of 'the fellas'. Jon watched as Tommy opened up Jamie O'Halloran's door and entered the room. Suddenly, Jon could hear noise coming from Jamie's room, as if furniture were being moved. After a few minutes, the noise stopped, except the rap music playing on Tommy's boom box. Moments later, Jamie's door opened, and Tommy exited.

Once again, the boom box was on his shoulder and Tommy's walk was slow and relaxed. Tommy looked towards Jon's door and spotting Jon, nodded his head. Jon nodded back and closed his door.

The phone in Jon's room rang. The ring was one short burst. This ring signaled that the call was coming from somewhere on the campus. Jon, who had been working on homework for his International Law class, paused and picked up the receiver.

"Yeah?"

"Quest?"

"Yeah?!"

"This is Stan . . ."

"Look Stan, this is study period and I'm at a really crucial part . . ."

"Yeah, all right. Anyway, I need to see you in my room at 10:30."

"Why?"

"Just be here."

"I ain't no toad, Stan. If you want to see me, tell me what you want."

"I want to talk to you about Friday's parade."

"What about it?"

"Be here at 10:30 and we'll talk then. Oh, by the way, it won't be necessary for you to bring any of your 'brothers.'"

"Stan, my momma only has one son," Jon shot back as he hung up the receiver. "Ugghh! Damn he gets on my last nerve!"

"What now?" asked Tyrone.

"Stan wants to see me at 10:30 to talk about Friday's parade."

"Well, it's not like you didn't expect it."

"Yeah, you're right. But I figured he would have said something on Friday or yesterday."

"Oh well. Massah's callin. Bettah git tah steppin!" said Tyrone.

———————

Jon walked down the gally to the corner room. He paused and looked at his watch. 10:30. He stood silent and waited. A few seconds later a trumpet blasted a single note over the PA system. This note signified the end of mandatory study period. Jon knocked on the door as he pushed it open. As he walked in, Jon was totally surprised to see the band director, Major Tyler Newman, standing in the room.

Major Newman was an impressive man. He was 6'2", with silver hair and a leathery face. He was a retired Marine and everything about him was witness to that fact. Major Newman always wore starched and pleated uniforms and was definitely no nonsense. Jon respected the major tremendously and he was one person with whom Jon was not particularly anxious to tangle.

"C'mon in Quest," said Stan, smiling.

Walking toward the corner where Stan and the major were standing, Jon stiffened. "Good evening, Sir," Jon said, addressing Major Newman.

"Good evening, Mr. Quest, sit down" Stan replied coldly.

"I'd rather stand, thank you."

"Suit yourself. We called you here today to talk to you about what happened at parade on Friday."

"Parade? Friday? I'm not sure I know what you are talking about. I wasn't at the parade," said Jon, feigning ignorance.

"Look, Quest," said Stan, turning red and raising his voice, "I ain't in the mood for games. You are well aware of what I'm talking about!"

"Why don't you refresh my memory?" Jon said defiantly.

"I'll refresh your memory . . ." Major Newman boomed.

Major Newman's outburst caught Jon, who had temporarily forgotten Major Newman was in the room, totally off guard.

". . . when we made our final turn, everyone's instrument went up to play the school fight song. Everyone's, that is, except the members of the Black Students Association. All their instruments remained at attention. *Now* do you remember?!"

"Well, Sir. With all due respect, 'Dixie' is not the school fight song," Jon said calmly.

"Look, Jon, regardless of whether it is the school fight song or not, it's what we always play," said Stan.

"Yeah, so?"

"So, why did you tell your members not to play?"

Jon looked blankly at Stan. Stan was standing in front of him with his face the color of a beet. His fists were clenched and a blue vein in his neck was bulging. Jon then looked at Major Newman. The major's icy blue eyes were piercing. His look was cold and hard.

Jon smiled to himself as he thought about the members of the BSA who had carried out the mission, exactly as planned.

Jon had anticipated this confrontation, though he had not anticipated the major's involvement. However, standing in Stan's room, he understood that he should have anticipated the major's involvement.

Valuable lessons are often learned in the midst of fire, Jon thought to himself.

Jon really liked the major. He really respected him for his professional talents, for his leadership, for what he had done to improve the band program at the M.U.T.S. However, he could not back down on his stance, even if the major was involved.

Jon had calculated the pros and cons of the situation prior to advising any of his officers or members. Jon had calculated everything from day one of the "incident." He had decided, as he had told the BSA, that the lines would be drawn, and everyone would have to pick sides. There would be no such thing as undecided. There would be no such thing as neutral. Major Newman's presence validated this fact. However, Jon knew that in war, there were always casualties.

"How do you know I told them to do anything?" queried Jon.

"You think we don't know about everything you do? You think we don't know you told them to sit when it is played at the games? You think we don't know you told them not to sing it when upperclassmen tell them to? You think we don't know? Yeah, we know. We didn't think they'd be dumb enough to do it, though. But we heard you told them not to worry. You told them if anyone asked, to tell them you told them to do it and you would deal with the heat!"

Jon felt the blood rush to his head.

Why Black people always gotta sell each other out? It could not have been anyone White because there were only bruthas in the room when I told them that, Jon thought.

"Look, Jon," said Major Newman, calmly. "Whatever is going on between the BSA and the administration has nothing to do with the band. It was unfair of you to combine the two."

"Major, what is going on is going on between the BSA and the entire university. We object to having to sing and play such a racist song. I don't wish I was in the land of cotton!"

"Jon, it is just a song," said Major Newman.

"Yeah and the KKK is just a social club!"

The major glared at Jon for a moment. Jon glared back.

There will be no intimidation here this evening! If you want to talk to me about something, then let's hear it, thought Jon.

"Yeah, I told them not to play, or sing, or stand. I told them and I am not taking it back! If you don't like it . . . pray, you'll get over it! But I gotta do what I feel is best for me and my organization."

"What about what is best for the band? What about loyalty to your company? What about esprit de corps?" demanded Stan.

"Look, I was Black before I was at this school or in this band! My loyalty is to my race. Now, if you plan on doing something to me, fine. You've been screwing me since I got here . . . don't stop now!"

"What does that mean, mister!" said Stan.

Jon, gritting his teeth, waved Stan off.

"I gotta be going. Is there anything else, Sir?"

"Yes, Jon, there is. How about a compromise?"

"Compromise?" said Jon, turning toward the major.

"Yes, on Friday there was a three-star Marine Corps General visiting. He noticed the cadets who did not raise their instruments. He asked the General about it. It was most embarrassing having our dirty laundry aired in public. We had thought that your absence at the parade would cause the cadets to forget or not want to do as you had instructed. That is why Colonel Henderson called you to his office, then excused you from the parade. So, if you and your cadets are going to continue with this . . ."

"And we are, Sir."

"Then could you at least have them bring their instruments up to the playing position? They don't have to play; all they have to do is bring their instruments up and act like they're playing. Finger some notes, take some breaths, etc."

Jon thought for a moment. He was not going to sell his guys out. Then again, he wanted to fight an effective battle. This meant concentrating attention on the most important areas.

"All right, major. This is the deal. We will bring our instruments up. We will not put them in our mouths, finger any notes, or take any fake breaths. I will tell you, Sir, I only do that much out of my respect and admiration for you."

The major looked at Stan. Stan looked back at the major with an expectant look on his face.

"Okay, Jon, deal," the major said with a sigh.

"May I be excused now, Sir?"

"Yes, Jon, that is all."

Jon looked at Stan, rolled his eyes toward the ceiling, and walked out of the room. Once on the galley, Jon breathed a loud, long sigh. As he walked back to his room, he smiled to himself. He had won that battle. It had been a battle with a formidable opponent. Nevertheless, he had won. There would be many more of those battles. However, Jon did not expect to win every one. But he knew he must win the majority of them in order to win this war.

CHAPTER 16

It was Friday night, and Jon and Tyrone were waiting in their room for McKenzie and Adam. The four were going to a high school football game in town. As they waited, they talked about the upcoming weekend. Tyrone was in the middle of a story about a girl he was planning on seeing when McKenzie walked into the room.

"Yeah, yeah, yeah. Whatever you're saying is a lie and we all know it. I could hear yo' black ass all the way down the galley! Why you gotta be so damn niggrish? Shit!" McKenzie stopped fussing long enough to cock his head to the side and contort his face.

"Is that Boone's Farm I smell?"

"Ummmmm, could be, and, could be not! Who's to say?" said Jon playfully. "Depends on whether you da brotha man or da otha man! If you da otha man, it's my new cologne. If you da brotha man, den you Got Damn Skippy, it's Boone's Farm!"

"Oh, I don't know, Jon. He looks like he could be de otha man disguised as de brotha man. Better not tell him anything!" chuckled Tyrone.

"Well, I can tell you without any hesitation that if I were the otha man, I would definitely be someplace else. I would be somewhere getting' a tan, havin' a brewski, countin' my money, or takin' some penis growth hormones!" joked McKenzie.

For several minutes, the three cadets howled in laughter.

"Damn, what the hell is so funny?" said Adam as he entered the room.

"Nuttin', man. You had to be there," said Jon, wiping the tears from him eyes and trying to stop laughing. "You want a drink?" Jon held out the bottle of strawberry wine toward Adam.

Adam took the bottle and began to drink. The other three cadets watched in amusement as the wine disappeared into Adam's mouth. Adam emptied the bottle and placed it loudly on the desk. He then looked around at the others, smiled, patted his stomach, then let out a loud belch. "Ahhhhh, that hit the spot," he said.

"Damn!" said McKenzie, shaking his head.

"Hey, don't worry about it, Adam, I didn't want anymore, you selfish bastard!" chided Tyrone.

"Well, you know when we open that stuff, we gotta finish it right then. If we don't finish it right then, it gets dangerous. I'm just trying to keep yo' big round head outta trouble." Turning to Jon, Adam pleaded for sympathy. "See what gratitude I get for trying to help out my little bruthas! I'm just too nice, that's my problem."

"You guys ready to roll?" asked Jon.

"Yeah."

"Uh huh."

"Let's roll!"

"Tyrone, you drivin'?"

"Like I have a choice. I'm the only one who has a car we can all fit in."

"We can all fit in mine," joked Jon.

"Yeah, right. Let's all go ride in Jon's car. Adam and McKenzie can ride in the back. Just open the hatch and shove them in. Oh, and don't worry about me, I'll just squeeze into the front . . . somehow. Shit, Jon, you know only one and a half people can ride in yo' 'Z'!" said Tyrone emphatically.

The cadets laughed heartily.

"I don't know what you're laughing at," McKenzie said to Adam. "Other than the fact that his is black and gold and yours is champagne, you two have the same damn car!"

"Let's go y'all," insisted Jon. "I would like to catch some of the game."

"To the Hoop de Mobile!" yelled Tyrone.

The four cadets walked out of Jon and Tyrone's room and exited the barracks. Once outside, they headed to the sophomore parking lot. A few minutes later, the cadets were climbing into Tyrone's car.

"Now, Tyrone, you ain't too fucked up to drive, are you? I don't wanna die tonight," said McKenzie, sarcastically.

"Man, you know good and got damn well I've been a lot worse off than this and got us where we were going!" Tyrone said indignantly, starting his car. Tyrone drove out of the parking lot and headed for town. At the front gate, he flashed the guard a toothy grin and waved. As he drove, the cadets laughed and talked about a party which was to take place the next day. Fifteen minutes later, Tyrone pulled his car into a vacant lot. The lot was used for parking during the high school home football games. Tyrone parked and the cadets hopped out of the car.

"Did y'all notice that car that kept passing us, then getting in front of us and slowing down?" asked McKenzie.

"Yeah, it was prolly jus' some punks from town. I didn't really pay no mind to 'em though."

"Yo' man. Is that one little honey that works at the mall gonna be here tonight?" Adam asked Jon.

"I dunno," shrugged Jon.

The cadets walked down a two-lane road which was lined on both sides with cars. They walked as close to the cars as possible, as they were talking towards oncoming traffic. Jon led the way and Tyrone brought up the rear. They had to yell to hear one another over the traffic. As they walked, a car heading in the same direction as they walked, slowed as it approached them. The car drove past them slowly and the four cadets could see figures inside the car watching them.

"Yo' Jon, who is that?" inquired Adam.

"I can't tell," said Jon.

"I don't recognize the car," said Tyrone.

"They look White," observed McKenzie.

Suddenly the car's tires squealed as the driver pressed hard on the accelerator. "Niggers!"

"Fuck you!" Adam shot back as he extended his middle finger high into the air.

The other three cadets, almost in unison, had also extended their middle fingers into the air in response to the driver's verbal attack.

"Man, White people are so damn ignorant!" said McKenzie in disgust.

"Yeah, and cowardly," agreed Jon.

"And they talk about us . . . phew!" sighed Tyrone.

"Yo' man, fuck them little bitches," said Adam, waving them off with his hand.

The cadets continued walking. Suddenly, Jon spotted the same car headed toward them. The car was riding as far on the shoulder as the parked cars would allow and was picking up speed.

"Hey, Jon!" yelled McKenzie, spotting the car.

"Man, we better get outta the way! That crazy son of a bitch is trying to run us over!" yelled Adam.

"Where the fuck we gonna go? These cars are bumper to bumper!" yelled Tyrone, frantically.

"Jump on a car or roll under one. Whatever you do, just get the fuck out the way!" yelled Jon as he leaped onto the hood of a parked car.

The oncoming car sideswiped the car Jon had leaped on and swerved back out onto the road. The car then stopped and started backing up. Jon, Tyrone, McKenzie, and Adam had all gotten off the hoods of the cars they had jumped on to avoid being run over and started running toward the car. A person on the passenger side stuck his head out the window and yelled at the cadets, "You black coons! You been causing too much trouble at the M.U.T.S.! You better shut up or next time, we'll finish the job!"

Dust and rocks sprayed the four cadets as the car sped off. The four cadets, who had been within a stone's throw of the car when it sped off, stood for a moment gasping for breath and watching the car disappear.

"Shit!" said Tyrone, who was leaning over with his hands on his knees.

"Did you get a look at the guy?" Jon asked through measured breaths.

"Naw."

"Did you?" Jon asked, turning to Adam.

"Naw, but I got the license plate number!" panted Adam.

"It was a red '5.0'!" proclaimed Tyrone, proudly.

"Yeah, I know," said Jon.

"We need to report this to the cops," remarked Tyrone.

"They ain't gonna care that some redneck White boys from town tried to run down four Black cadets! Get real! The majority of the boys in this town, White and Black, are jealous of us anyway," responded Adam.

"Fellas," said McKenzie quietly.

The other cadets looked at McKenzie curiously. Each was wondering why he was so quiet. Was he hurt? Was he still getting over the scare?

"What?" they all said, almost in unison.

"Those guys were cadets."

"Cadets!?" said Tyrone in disbelief.

"Get the fuck outta here," answered Adam.

"How do you know?" asked Jon.

"There was a parking sticker on their bumper," McKenzie said.

"Yeah, well that doesn't prove anything," insisted Tyrone.

"There were summer leave uniform hats in the back window."

"Yeah, well maybe they know some cadets or something. That still don't prove anything," insisted Tyrone.

"I recognize the car and I recognize the guy who yelled out the window. I've seen him before on the yard. They were the same ones who kept getting in front of us and cutting us off on the way over here."

"You don't know that for—" began Tyrone.

"Shut up, Tyrone!" commanded Jon.

"You've got to be kidding me," said Adam quietly.

"I wish I were," McKenzie said.

"Man, I don't know about y'all, but I ain't much in the mood to be around a bunch of people tonight," said Tyrone.

"Me neither," agreed Adam.

"Let's go get some Private Stock, some Pink Champale, and some Boone's Farm and roll up to the Activity Center at City College. If ain't nuthin' up, we'll roll down to Northern College and see what's up there," said Jon.

"I'm with that," said Tyrone, eagerly.

"Bet!" said Adam. "C'mon, McKenzie, let's go."

The cadets walked back to the vacant lot where Tyrone had parked. As they crossed the dimly lit lot, a shot rang out. The cadets immediately dove for cover. The bullet hit a car window behind them. They put their arms over their heads as they heard the glass shatter. A second later, another shot rang out. This bullet ricocheted off a car door. Another shot rang out and once again, they heard glass shatter.

"Yo' fuck this! I ain't laying here and waiting for somebody to come kill me!" said Jon as he began crawling toward Tyrone's car.

The other cadets were also on the move. Each one headed for Tyrone's car. Tyrone arrived first and reached up and unlocked the front door, opened it, and crawled in. Keeping low, he unlocked the other doors and waited as the other three crawled in. After making sure everyone was in, he started his car.

On the outside, there was silence. The cadets listened intently as they huddled out of sight. The shooting had stopped. They could not hear anything or anyone.

"Yo, man, get us the hell outta here!" demanded Adam in a fierce whisper.

As Tyrone put his car in reverse and peeped over the seat, another shot rang out. Almost instantly, Tyrone's right side-view mirror shattered.

"Fuck you!" Tyrone yelled as he sat up in his seat and slammed on the accelerator. The car jerked backward. Tyrone slammed on the brakes, threw the car into drive, and pressed hard on the accelerator again. The car swerved and fishtailed, then straightened, as Tyrone gained control.

Outside the car, the cadets could hear several more shots. They heard one or two of them as they struck the car.

"Quest, we're gonna kill you and your nigger friends!" came a warning from the dark of the vacant lot.

For several minutes, the four cadets, who were each sweating profusely, said nothing. Each sat mopping his face and staring out his respective window. After about five minutes, Jon broke the silence.

"Hey, Tyrone."

"Yeah?"

"Forget the liquor, let's just go back to campus. Adam, if you or McKenzie want Tyrone to drop you somewhere . . ."

"Nah, I just wanna get back to my cell block," said Adam quietly.

"Ditto," agreed McKenzie.

The cadets rode the remainder of the way to the campus in silence. Each of them was deep in thought. Each of them was still shaken. As they walked toward their barracks, Jon outlined the next steps.

"Tomorrow, we will meet at fifteen hundred at the Public Safety office to report this. Adam, make sure you write down the license number, so you don't forget it."

Adam nodded his head in acknowledgment. At the entrance of Tyrone and Jon's barracks, Jon stopped and turned to Tyrone, Adam, and McKenzie.

"You know what this means?" he queried. "It means they are serious. We've gotten to them. I mean really gotten to them. There is no turning back now. We have to recognize that a lot of White people would rather kill or be killed than face up to their ignorance. We have to be just as committed and determined. Intimidation, harassment, threats, violence. None of it is great enough to divert us from our goal. That's the only way it can be. When we can trust no one, we must be able to trust one another."

Jon paused and looked at his friends. He studied each of them for a moment.

"You realize they won't stop until we're all either run out of here or dead. That ain't no joke either. If you don't believe me, look at your uniforms and look at Tyrone's side mirror. So, make up your minds now. If you want to back out, now is the time. We're all targets. I'm a central target. Adam is a central target. Everyone else is a target by association. But whether by design or association, you are still a target. And don't fool yourselves, you'll be just as dead whether by design or otherwise!"

Jon paused and looked at his friends and a sad look came across his face.

"I'm sorry for getting all of you into this."

Jon turned and walked into his barracks and headed for his room.

CHAPTER 17

"Wow, Jon!" exclaimed Marcus. "Man, I had no idea! Fights, threats, guns!"

"I know! Man, I don't know how you were able to study, let alone graduate," agreed Angelo.

Jon looked at his two brothers-in-law and smiled. "It wasn't easy."

"Yeah, we had to keep him focused," interjected Kathy with a smile. "He would call me sometimes, babbling and sounding like a scatterbrain. We told him he needed to talk to someone."

"Yeah, the Lord!" interrupted Jon Sr., sitting up in his chair.

Kathy shot a look at Jon Sr. He looked at Kathy, then settled back into his chair, mumbling to himself.

"Anyway," continued Kathy, "there were days when we prayed harder than others. Trust me, none of those White folks down there were any happier to see Jon Jr. go than we were."

"I know, that's right," chuckled Joyell. "He used to write me letters and tell me about some of the things he was going through. I was always really scared for him."

"Yeah, me too," agreed Bernice. "That's why Joy and I cheered so hard and loud when he walked across the stage to get his degree. In fact, we were the only ones who cheered at all!"

"You're kidding," insisted Marcus.

"No, for real. Everyone else hissed," beamed Bernice.

Jon was quiet. He looked from person to person as they spoke. It interested him that after all these years his family was still passionate about that part of his life. He remembered feeling so alone while he was going through it all. The majority of the cadets in the BSA were afraid to go beyond a certain point. They were afraid to really challenge the "system." Understandably so, because for the ones who did, the consequences were often severe.

"You've got to be kidding!" Jon said in astonishment.

The voice on the other end of the phone was calm and low.

"Adam, man, you can't go out like that!"

"Jon, they were gonna kick me out. At least they gave me a choice."

"A choice! Some fuckin' choice! Resign or be expelled! That ain't no fuckin' choice! Who did this?"

"Well, the first sergeant approached me."

"Tell me again what he said. There has to be something we can do."

"Jon, we've been over this shit before and it's no use . . ."

"Tell me again, Goddammit!"

"The first sergeant came to my room right after muster and said I went AWOL the night before. Then he asked me if I had. Of course, I said no. He said okay and walked away like no big deal. Next thing I know, our Honor Court rep is in my room with two other guys. They told me they knew I had gone AWOL the night before and had just denied it to the first sergeant. Therefore, I was being brought up on the Honor Court charge of lying. I told them I was not AWOL, I was in 'AB's' room. They looked me in my eyes and said they knew exactly where I was, but it didn't matter. They said they were bringing me up on the charges and there was nothing I could do about it. They said there was nothing anyone could do to help me. They told me even you and your vigilante squad could not help me. Therefore, I should just go ahead and resign. They told me if I didn't, they'd kick me out and I'd lose all my college credits. Jon, you know as well as I do ain't no brutha ever gone up before the Honor Court and been found innocent."

"Yeah, I know. But what about 'AB,' can't he testify for you?"

"They already got to him. They told him they would kick him off the football team and pull his scholarship if he so much as cleared his throat. And that would be just for starters."

"Damn!"

"Jon, I got no choice. You know they're gonna win if I try to fight. If I get expelled, they'll destroy all my records and I'll have to start all over again somewhere else. I can't go through with all of that. I just can't, man, it ain't worth it. At least this way, I haven't thrown away three years of my life. I mean, c'mon, cuz, what would you do?"

"I would fight to the end," Jon said quietly.

"Yeah, that's what you say now because it ain't your nuts in the vice. Things change when it's your life they're talking about fuckin' up. I got my future to think about. This shit just ain't worth it."

"Ain't worth it?! What about everything we've done? What about everything we've been through? Was it all for nothing?"

"Look, Jon, fuck the speeches. Don't pull that rah-rah bull-shit on me. I ain't the one! I'm leavin' Goddammit! I'm going in this week, taking my finals, then packin' up my shit and gettin' the hell outta this place. And no, I ain't lookin' back! They won't get me! Don't you remember what happened to Hal?"

"Yeah, I do."

"Hal tried to fight. The first time they tried to kick him out on homosexuality charges, remember? They said someone caught him smokin' cheeba and giving head to a janitor in the bell tower."

"Yeah, Adam, I remember. That was such bullshit!"

"Damn right it was! Hal wasn't no faggot! You and I both know that! But it was a good way to kick him out and excommunicate him at the same time. I mean, they wouldn't have to prove anything. All they had to do was accuse him."

"Yeah, but they didn't expect him to fight."

"Neither did he. Look, Jon, Hal was my room dog. He was gonna just leave. But me with my big mouth. I ran that same rah-rah bullshit line on him that you ran on me. He listened. Some days I wish I would've just shut up and let him go."

"Adam, you can't blame yourself for what happened to Hal!"

"Why not? If I wouldn't have opened my mouth and convinced him to fight, he'd be alive today!"

"Look, Adam, after they convicted him of that Honor Code violation, we all knew he was upset. I mean, he was devastated. After all the time he had been here, what, five years? After he disappeared, we all suspected the worse . . ."

"No, we all suspected foul play," interrupted Adam.

"Yeah, yeah. Same, same. My point is no one ever blamed you. When they found him, we all knew he hadn't committed suicide. We knew."

"Hell, yeah we knew! Don't no niggah commit suicide!!!"

"But regardless of whether it was suicide or foul play, the fault is not yours. If there is fault, it is fault by association. The fact that he was your room dog, you were involved with the BSA, and more so, the fact that you all are associated with me, is why this is all happening. If anyone should feel responsible, it should be me!"

". . . and you should. This is all your fault! And I ain't lettin' you fuck up my life so you can have your name in lights!"

The words cut through Jon like a hot knife through warm butter. For a moment there was a thick and uncomfortable silence.

Jon sat with his heart in his mouth and tears in his eyes. He realized at that point how this struggle was affecting his friends. After what seemed like hours, Adam began to speak again.

"Hey, man, I'm sorry. I didn't mean those things. I shouldn't have said them. I wasn't trying to hurt you."

"Yeah, well the truth hurts," Jon said quietly.

"Look, Jon, the fact of the matter is that if I would'a just let Hal go, it probably wouldn't have happened. But anyway, my mind is set. After finals, I'm outta here!"

Jon was quiet for a moment. He sat motionless with the phone to his ear.

"Jon?" Silence. "Jon!"

"Good luck, man. I'm gonna miss you."

"Thanks. I'll miss you too. But I won't miss this!"

"Where are you gonna go next?"

"I dunno, maybe Morgan State. Maybe Delaware State. Who knows? Maybe I'll take a break for a while. I need to get myself together."

"Well, whatever you do, do me a favor . . ."

"What?"

"First, lay off the hard stuff."

"Yeah, and second?"

"Get some professional help."

"And . . .?"

"Finally, wax some northern ass for me."

"That goes without saying."

"Yeah, I figured that one would," said Jon, smiling.

"Good luck, Jon. Man, don't be crazy. Don't be bull-headed and stay around here 'til they kill yo' black ass. They been tryin'. Sooner or later, yo' luck is gonna run out!"

"Yeah, well let's hope it runs out later and not sooner."

"Yeah, let's hope . . ."

There was a long, awkward pause as both cadets searched for the appropriate words. Adam's search ended first.

"Jon."

"Yeah?"

"You've been like a brother to me. We've shared some good times and some bad. We have been friends and enemies. I'll never forget the good times. I am sorry for the bad. Some days I look back and regret that we locked horns over a female. But through all of that, I'll never forget you, man. Never."

"Hey, dog," Jon said, fighting back tears, "if I could do it all over again, I am not sure of everything I would change, but I know I would do things differently where you and I are concerned. You mean a lot to me, Adam. From the day we met, you and I connected, more so than anyone else. I am sorry we let other people break up a friendship like that. Life is too short to let a good friend go by the wayside. I'll never forget what we shared. I'll never forget the good times. I'll never forget the first time Jace took us out to Waynesboro and the Kappas and the Qs got in a fight in that gym. We wanted to jump in so bad. Jace wouldn't let us, though. After that we left and went and got drunk. Remember when we came back to campus and had to run back to our rooms? We were so fucked up! We could barely stand up, much less run. Oh! Man, we had some good times. I'll always remember the good times. As far as the bad times . . . what bad times?"

"Jon, if you ever need anything . . . !"

"Yeah man, I know. I can call you. The same goes for you."

"Bet!"

"Look, Adam, I gotta go," sniffled Jon. "Keep your head up. I don't know if I'll see you before you go . . . But hey, don't worry, everything is gonna be alright. It's all good. You're doin' the right thing."

"I know I am." Adam paused and then said, "But Jon . . ."

"Yeah?"

"So are you."

"Thanks, man. Thanks for the support. Thanks for everything!"

Jon hung up the phone and sat motionless as tears met under his chin.

"Jon, you alright? What's up?" asked Tyrone as he walked in the room and noticed tears streaming down his roommate's face.

"Nuthin'," said Jon as he quickly dried his face with his palms and tried to regain his composure.

"Yeah, right! What's up for real. You're sittin' there like a bump on a log, like your girl just told you she got clap or some shit."

Tyrone snickered and Jon forced a smile. "Adam is resigning."

"What? Why?!"

"They brought him up on an Honor Court violation. Then they told him he could resign, or they'd kick him out. So, he resigned. He's gonna finish his exams then transfer."

"Deep!"

"I know."

"Ain't that the same shit they did to Hal?"

"Yeah, real similar."

"Ya know, Jon, when they found Hal dead, that scared the hell out of me. I mean, I knew then that they weren't playin'. Look at it though, man. We been run off the road. We been almost run down on several occasions. We been shot at several times. I still haven't fixed the bullet holes in my hoopty. We have guys coming in here almost daily talking noise. And how many times in the middle of the night have you and I had to fight people who sneak in here to give us a blanket party? I mean we sleep with clubs under our pillows, for Christ's sake! When does it all end? Where does it all end? Yo, 'G,' these crackahs are serious. They're sending a message. They're saying that don't no niggah rock their boat . . . and if one does, they'll make his ass walk the plank!"

"Calm down, Tyrone. We can't afford to lose our heads. Not now. Not as long as we are here."

"No!!! Tell that shit to Hal and his people. Jon, after Hal got kicked out, we all thought it was over. All of us, that is, except Mr. Whitey. Jon, they went after him after he left. Man, I used to think once one of us resigned or got kicked out, that'd be it. It'd be over. Bullshit!!! Man, it ain't over 'til they totally break you or kill you! One or the other . . . or both!" Tyrone said hysterically.

Jon looked at Tyrone as he paced back and forth across the room. Tyrone was noticeably upset and agitated. Jon hadn't seen his roommate like this before. Normally, Tyrone was laid back. Lately, however, he was more and more agitated and nervous. Tyrone's change in behavior worried Jon.

"Tyrone, calm down. The last thing I need is for my room dog to go to pieces on me," Jon said calmly.

Tyrone continued pacing and wringing his hands.

Jon looked at his roommate and shook his head. *What is this place doing to us?* he thought.

The stress, the constant danger they were all under. The constant harassment. The constant threat of violence. Although they hid it well, they were all on the verge of losing their minds. They could barely study. Concentration on any one thing was almost impossible. It was a wonder they had not all flunked out. It was a wonder they had anything: sanity, peace of mind, passing grades, relationships, anything.

"Geez, now with Adam leaving, it feels like we are dropping like flies. It makes you wonder who is next?!", lamented Jon.

"Me, Jon," said Tyrone quietly.

"What'd you say?" said Jon, jumping up from his desk.

"I said me. I am not coming back next year. I was gonna tell you later, but now's as good a time as any."

"Yeah, right, Tyrone. Quit playin'," said Jon.

"I ain't playin', Jon. Look, man, my grades are sucking wind. I got a phone call the other night. The person on the other end told me if I promise to leave after this year, then I'll pass everything. If not, I'd be lucky to get an 'F' average this semester. So . . . I promised. They told me that reneging on my word could be fatal. The next day, my professor in calculus changed my grade from an F to a B-. He said he had gone back and regraded some of my tests and noticed he had made some mistakes during the grading. He said he felt I did have a grasp on what was going on. Jon, I ain't about to hang around while they ruin my life. I'm here on a full math scholarship, Jon, and I can't afford to lose that due to bad grades. I'm scared, man. Man, back in D.C., I roam the streets and ain't scared of nobody or nuthin'. But here, I can't see my enemies. I don't know who is and who isn't okay. Jon, I don't need this. I have to graduate. They told me if I transfer, then my scholarships would follow me. But, if I don't, I would lose everything. Jon, my family is depending on me. Don't make this hard on me. Please understand."

Hal flashed across Jon's mind. The conversation with Adam flashed across Jon's mind. The comments Adam had made flashed across Jon's mind.

"I do understand," Jon said quietly. "Really, I do."

"Man!" said Angelo. He let out a long whistle and rolled his eyes toward the ceiling. "That's deep!"

"Jon, you da man," Marcus said as he raised his coffee cup in tribute.

"To this day, I still don't know how he managed to deal with all of that, plus study, plus do all his extracurriculars," said Joyell. "When I was in college, it was all I could do to make it to class!"

Bernice nodded her head emphatically.

"Yeah, well to this day, I still don't understand why it was so tough for you to make it to class. You didn't have any children, didn't have a job, wasn't involved in any extracurriculars and yet you couldn't even get out of the bed in the morning."

"Yeah, right," laughed Jon. "As if she got that way when she got to college. She was that way before she left home! I mean the maid would always have to wake her up. What was that maid's name anyway?"

"Yvette," said Joyell, dryly. "She didn't have to wake me all the time. Uh, we're not here to talk about my past sleeping habits! And Bernice, I know the pot ain't calling the kettle black!"

"Yeah, anyway," said Marcus. "What happened your senior year? Did your roommate really leave? Did the death threats continue? Did they ever prove Hal was murdered?"

"Calm down, Marc," said Bernice with a disapproving scowl. "The story ain't all that! After all, he is sitting here talking about it and not in Hollywood making sequels! God!"

"Gee, thanks Bernice. I guess that settles everything. End of story. Now why don't you just wander outside and have a puff," said Joyell, sarcastically.

Bernice, with daggers in her eyes, turned to Joyell.

"I don't puff anymore. I haven't for a long time. I'm saved and have received my deliverance . . . *et tu?*" said Bernice.

"Go ahead, Jon, continue," Kathy cut in. "Lawd have mercy!"

Jon looked at Kathy and smiled, then looked around the room. Bernice and Joyell were still glaring at each other. Lexie sat patiently and quietly, waiting for Jon to continue his story. He turned and looked out the window. For a moment, there was complete silence. Suddenly, as if hit by a creative thought, Jon whirled around and began talking . . .

CHAPTER 18

J on sat in his room, looking around. *One more year!* he thought. Finally, in his senior year, Jon had the mental and psychological scars to prove he had been involved in a protracted war. It seemed that he had dealt with disappointments, crises, and challenges for three straight years. Now, he could almost see the light at the end of the tunnel. He was almost home!

Over the summer, Jon fractured the tibia of his left leg while away at Marine Corps Officer Candidate School. He returned for his senior year with a full cast on his left leg. As Jon sat on his bed, he stared at the big, bulky item attached to his leg. *Great!* he thought. *Now I'm a sitting duck for whoever comes after me. It's not like I have Tyrone to help me anymore.*

"Knock, knock. Anybody home?" came a voice from outside the door.

Jon looked up as Aaron Harris, one of his senior classmates, entered his room.

Aaron was one of the few White cadets with whom Jon was still friendly. Aaron was attending the M.U.T.S. on an Air Force Pilot Scholarship and was an electrical engineering major. Aaron had a brilliant mind and was phenomenal with numbers. The problem with Aaron was that as brilliant as his mind was, his personality was equally as repulsive and annoying to most other cadets. His irritating personality made it difficult for him to make and keep friends. He liked Jon because Jon accepted him as he was. He liked the fact that Jon didn't belittle him or make him feel less than a person.

"Hey, bro'," said Aaron, holding out his hand so Jon could give him five.

Jon looked at Aaron's hand as if he had just taken it out of a pile of crap. "Aaron, how many times do I have to tell you that Black people don't do that anymore! Geez!"

"Oh yeah," Aaron said apologetically.

"Yeah, well, just try to remember next time. Now, what can I do for you?"

"I need to talk to you."

"About what?"

"About your roommate."

"My roommate? I don't have a roommate."

"Exactly. I was wondering . . ."

"Now, Aaron, look . . ."

"Aw, just hear me out, Jon. I won't be a problem. I promise. I will be quiet . . ."

"You? Quiet?"

"No, really, I will. You won't even know I'm here. I go over to the E-E hall every night to study, so you'll have the room to yourself. I won't be any problem, Jon! Please!"

"Why?"

"Why?"

"Yeah, why? Why *my* roommate?"

"Well, Jon, you know I think you're a great guy. I mean you're really cold with me."

"Cool."

"What?"

"Really *cool* with me."

"Yeah, exactly."

"Who sent you?"

"Who sent me?! Nobody sent me. I'm here on my own. I promise. I won't get in the way of you or any of your Black friends. I mean you can hold meetings here and everything. As a matter of fact, I have been wanting to ask you about becoming a member of the Black Students Association."

"Whoa, whoa! First things first. Truth be told, you want to come here because nobody else will room with you. Right?"

"No, not really. I mean I could've roomed by myself."

"Then why don't you?"

"Well, I, uh. Er uh . . . uh . . ."

"You're scared."

"What!?"

"Scared, you heard me. You think they'll really fuck with you if you are all alone. There is safety in numbers. If the Whites throw you out, go to the bruthas, they'll take care of you. Ain't that right?"

Aaron stood silently, staring at the floor.

Jon gave it some thought and with a sense of resignation, said, "Yeah, it's cool. You can move in tomorrow. I'll have my Platoon Sergeant draft up a platoon transfer tonight."

"Thank you, Jon!!! Thank you so much! You won't regret this."

"I better not," snarled Jon, his eyes piercing through Aaron.

Aaron cleared his throat, swallowed uncomfortably, and forced a smile. "You won't . . . I promise."

"Aaron," said Jon as he positioned himself to look directly at Aaron, "if you ever cross me, I won't regret it, but you will!"

Aaron looked at Jon and searched for a smile that wouldn't come. Finally, he forced an uneasy grin. Jon stared long and hard at his new roommate. His stare was icy, cold, and serious. After a few moments, he turned away.

"I'll see you tomorrow," Jon said with a smile.

"Uh, yeah, okay," said Aaron as he quickly exited the room. Jon turned and watched the screen door as it banged shut. *I wonder who is up to what now?*

Jon stood in front of his platoon and stared into the distance. He was waiting for his Platoon Sergeant to finish with attendance and report to him.

"Hey, dude . . ."

Jon turned toward the voice and noticed Richard Bolton as he approached him. Richard was Jon's company commander. He was also his roommate their sophomore year. Richard had advanced through the ranks quite successfully. He had phenomenal grades, almost a 3.8 average. However, militarily, he was not as sharp as Jon. Many people thought if Jon had not gotten involved in the BSA, he would have attained the highest rank out of any of the classmates in his company their senior year. But, because of his involvement and their desire to punish him, Richard was able to advance instead. Although the reason given to Jon for his low senior rank was his lack of academic strength.

Jon's grades had suffered ever since he became involved in the BSA. There was even an incident during his junior year when his grades were changed. Jon had picked his grades up prior to leaving for Christmas break. However, when his grades were sent home, they had all been lowered by one or two grades.

Upon returning from the break, Jon went to the dean of undergraduate studies and reported the incident. An investigation ensued. The end result, however, did not change. All the professors claimed they had to regrade all their final exams due to certain questions being unfair or having received reports of cheating. When they did, they felt Jon either cheated or did not have a true grasp of the material. It stunk to high heaven as far as Jon was concerned. All that aside, Jon still managed to be on the Dean's List and receive a departmental scholarship. But it certainly was not because they wanted to give him either.

However, whatever the reasons Jon did not advance through the military ranks, he still somehow kept good grades, was "sharp" on the military side, stayed out of trouble, and committed himself to the BSA. As a matter of a fact, it was this commitment which he believed caused his grades and military life to suffer. His former company commander had warned him that if he became too vocal or involved in the BSA, he would "jeopardize his military and academic success."

Just the same, Jon liked Richard. He thought Richard was a great guy and did not blame him for what had happened.

"So how do you like rooming with your loser of a roommate?" Richard queried Jon.

"Well any thing's better than that asshole I roomed with in my sophomore year," Jon said with a smile.

"How long has it been?" Richard said, ignoring Jon's remark. "One month? One year?" continued Richard with a wide grin.

"Yeah, it feels about like a month. It's okay. It's not too bad. He is gone every night during study period and our classes clash, so I'm generally not there when he is or vice versa."

"Man, I feel sorry for you! You're a good guy. I couldn't do it."

"Yeah, well like I said, he is rarely there when I am."

Suddenly over the loudspeaker, the voice of the Regimental Adjutant interrupted the exchange between Jon and his former roommate.

"Companies receive your reports!"

"Awright, Jon gotta run. Talk to ya later."

"Awright, Rich. See ya."

CHAPTER 19

Jon lay on his bed, reading. Outside his room, he heard several cadets laughing and talking. The voices sounded as if they were getting closer and coming toward Jon's room. Moments later, there was a knock as Jon's door swung open. Jon looked up as Tim, Evan, and McKenzie walked into his room.

"Uh yeah . . . come in," Jon said dryly.

"Well, thank you," retorted Evan.

"Hey, brothers!" said Aaron as he got up from his desk, crossed the room, and held out his hand for someone to give him five.

The three cadets looked at him, at his hand, at Jon, and finally at one another.

"Yeah, anyway," they said in unison and turned away.

"Sit yo' sorry white ass down," said McKenzie, smiling at Jon.

"Look, Jon, we need to talk to you . . . in private," said Tim.

"Well, let's not do it here," said Jon. "You know this room is probably bugged."

Jon pointed to Tim and motioned him closer. Jon circled his index finger and pointed up. The three shook their heads, turned, and exited the room.

"So, what did all of that mean?" inquired Aaron.

"If I wanted you and everybody else to know, I would have just said it," retorted Jon.

'Yeah, well, you can tell me . . . I am your roommate."

"Uh huh."

"What does that mean? Circle your wagons? Did it mean you're meeting in the lobby of a building? Are you meeting around a certain time, somewhere up in the student center? I'm sure it meant something."

"Aaron, it's a Black thing, you wouldn't understand. And besides, why are you asking so many questions, anyway?" Jon said, turning and fixing a stare on Aaron. He studied him for a moment. "Remember what I told you, Aaron?"

"Hey, Jon," Aaron said, forcing a laugh. "I was just wondering, that's all."

"That better be all!"

Jon rolled awkwardly out of his bed and looked around for his sneakers. Locating them in the corner of the room next to his desk, he wobbled over, sat down, and put one of them on. After a minute, and out of breath, Jon stood up and picked up his walking stick. Jon exited his room, walked to the far end of the barracks, and climbed four flights of stairs. Once on the fourth floor, Jon paused to catch his breath.

"God I hate this thing!" Jon said disgustedly, tapping his cast with his walking stick. "I'll be glad to get it off."

After collecting his breath, Jon walked to the area where "F" company lived, walked down two flights of stairs and over to Tim's room. Jon looked around, then knocked on the door.

"C'min."

Jon pushed the door open, walked in, and closed the door behind him. Once in the room, Jon let out a loud sigh. He looked around the room and noticed Tim sprawled out on the top bunk, Evan on the bottom, and McKenzie sitting at Tim's desk.

"Awright, fellas, whassup?"

"First of all," started McKenzie, "when are you gonna get rid of that dork you call a roommate? Geez! Es-tu stupide?"

"C'est possible! Mais je ne suis pas ici pour discuter de mon problème, d'accord?"

"Yeah, anyway!" said Evan impatiently.

"Oh, sorry guys," said McKenzie. "Jon, Tim has a great idea he wants to discuss with you."

"Okay, Tim. Let's hear it."

"Jon, you know all the problems we've been having with all the confederate flags at the games?"

"Yeah."

"Well, what if we give them something else to wave instead!"

"Uh huh, go ahead. Something else like what?"

"A towel."

"A towel?"

"Yeah, a towel with a big paw print on it. They can wave it at the games instead of the confederate flag."

"I like it. I like it. The Minnesota Twins had their 'Homer Hanky,' the Houston Oilers had their 'Terrible Towels' . . . now we have the . . . 'Tiger Towel'! I love it! Okay, now what are you tellin' me for? What do you want me to do to help?"

"Well, first of all, I don't have the connections to buy the towels or have them screened, but I know you do. Second of all, you have an avenue of advertising and distributing the towels. Third of all, you can help with the overall marketing of the idea. I mean, I came up with the idea, but I know you can make it work. I bounced it off Evan and McKenzie to see what they thought and to see if they thought you would like the idea. I figure we could split the profits four ways."

"Tim, it is a great idea and I have no doubt that Jon will cooperate fully. Ain't that right, frat?!" said McKenzie.

Jon looked at McKenzie with amusement.

"Geez, give a niggah a blazer and he thinks he runs the whole damn world," Jon said with a half laugh. Then turning to Tim, he continued. "Yeah, Tim, we can run with it. I'll tell you what, why don't you let me check on some things and we will meet in a couple of days and put this thing together. Let's plan to meet two days from today at 8:00, here in Tim's room. Okay?"

The other three cadets agreed. For several minutes, the four cadets stood around engaged in general conversation. Then noticing the time, they filtered out, one by one.

Two days later, Jon, Tim, Evan, and McKenzie met in Tim's room to put the 'Tiger Towel' concept together.

"First of all, we need to talk about the pricing strategy. The towels will cost about $.75 each. All totaled, each finished towel will cost $1.25. If we are going to use the BSA, they will need to get a cut. So, let's say, of the profit, they will get $1.00 from each towel sold. Agreed?"

Tim, Evan, and McKenzie all nodded in unison.

"Jon," said McKenzie, "I suggest we offer the towels in two different colors. We can offer it in navy blue with a burgundy imprint and in burgundy with a navy-blue imprint."

"That's a great idea," agreed Jon.

"But is that going to be an additional charge for the other color towel or ink?" asked Evan.

"No, it won't. It is all the same. The price only goes up if we do more than one color on the towel. Okay, what about distribution, Tim?" asked Jon.

"Well, I figured we could have BSA members go room to room in the barracks and sell the towels," stated Tim.

"Yeah, but that isn't allowed. Trust me, I know from experience. Remember last year when Tyrone and I were selling donuts and hot dogs and got caught?" interjected McKenzie.

"Yeah, well that is where Jon comes in. If he goes to Col. Ball and the General and sells these towels as relieving racial tension, then they will okay it." said Evan.

"Good thinking, Evan," said Tim.

"Okay, that's no problem. We can get the student paper to do an article on it also," said Jon.

"But what if the cadets don't buy off on it and sales aren't very good?" asked Evan.

"Well, what if the cadets do buy off on it and sales are phenomenal? But that aside, you have something in mind?" returned Jon.

"Yeah, I do. What if we introduce the towels at homecoming? Then sell the towels to the public. Make them available before the game. Jon, you can talk to your connections and get us some TV coverage. Which would mean free advertisement. We could sell a mint that way. Everyone would buy one!"

The room was suddenly buzzing with excitement. The cadets spoke excitedly about the number of towels they could sell. They talked about looking into the crowd and seeing all those towels waving. They talked about how much of an eyesore the confederate flags were. They talked about how negative a person would be perceived if they were waving the confederate flag as opposed to waving a towel. For more than five minutes, the cadets talked among themselves. Finally, however, Jon restored order.

"Fellas, fellas! Look, we have some great ideas. Now we have to get them done. All right, I will talk to the General about setting up a table and selling them for homecoming. But, before I do that, we need to take care of some other issues. How much do each of you think we should charge for each towel?"

"I say we charge $4.50," concluded McKenzie. "That will cover the cost of the towel, give us money to invest in more towels, and pay for gas and labor."

"That sounds good," said Evan, nodding his head in agreement.

"Yeah, it does. So, $4.50 it is," said Tim triumphantly.

Jon sat silently for a moment. As the others turned to look at him, they could tell he was deep in thought.

"Well . . . Jon?" prodded Evan.

"$4.50 won't work," said Jon finally.

"Why?" said McKenzie indignantly.

"Which of you is going to be responsible for making sure we have quarters or change all the time? Remember K-I-S-S?"

"Yeah, Kiss the Inside of . . ."

"Shut up, McKenzie," interrupted Evan.

"K-I-S-S. Keep It Simple Stupid," said Tim.

"Exactly. So, we need to keep it simple. So, we will charge five bucks per towel," concluded Jon. "Agreed?"

"No prob," said Evan.

"Agreed."

There was a pause as everyone waited for McKenzie to give his verbal approval.

McKenzie sat with his legs crossed, arms folded, looking at the ceiling. Finally, he nodded his head, as if it required extreme effort.

"Good. What we'll do is each of us will kick in twenty-five bucks to buy and imprint our initial supply. Tomorrow, I will call my girl over at the *Ebony Chronicle* newspaper—" said Jon.

"Wit' her fine self," interjected Tim.

"Yeah, anyway. I will call her and get her to do a story on the 'Tiger Towel.' Then I'll call Channel 7 and get them to come out and do a story on it. Then after that I will make an appointment to see the General. Now, Tim, I will need you to go with me to see the General and the reporters," stated Jon.

"No problem," beamed Tim.

"By the time we get in to see the General, there will have been a lot of coverage on this. Also, when we go in, we will take Tim so he can do a write-up on it in the school paper. So, do any of you have any questions?"

"Nope," said Tim, who was preoccupied with the PR side of the 'Tiger Towel.'

McKenzie shook his head slowly from side to side.

"Yeah, I do," said Evan. "How do you plan on incorporating the BSA into selling?"

"I don't."

"Excuse me?"

"We will do all the selling. The fewer hands that are in the cookie jar, the fewer cookies that come up missing. We will give them part of the proceeds. However, we will not use any of the members. The only ones who will sell these towels will be the four of us in this room now."

"Okay," said Evan, rubbing his chin with his index finger and thumb and nodding his head. "That makes sense."

"Anything else?" Jon inquired, looking from one cadet to another. Jon stood up and stretched. "Man!" he said. "I guess I'll see you fellas later." He bent over and began gathering his papers.

The other three cadets were standing and gathering their belongings by now as well.

"Oh yeah," said Jon as he opened the door, "everything we discussed needs to stay between us. We wouldn't want anyone else trying to capitalize on Tim's great ideas, would we?"

As Jon lay on his bed napping, the telephone rang. "Hello," said Aaron. "Yeah, hold on. Jon!"

"What?" Jon said groggily, rolling over on the bed.

"Phone. It's for you."

"Well, I'm trying to take a nap, Aaron. Who is it?"

"Who's calling?" asked Aaron on the phone. "Jon, I think you better get this."

"Why? Who is it?" Jon said impatiently.

"A reporter from *Athletics Illustrated*."

"Yeah, right! Hang up the phone, Aaron. I ain't in the mood for jokes."

"But what if it really—"

"Aaron, hang up the fuckin' phone, man. Don't you know when people are playing on the phone?"

"Sorry," Aaron said as he hung up the phone. "Jon, I'm going to work out. You wanna come?"

"No, Aaron. What I want to do is get some sleep! Do you mind?!"

"Touchy, touchy!" Aaron grabbed his racquetball racquet and headed out the door.

Several minutes later, the phone rang again.

"Aaron, get the phone, man," Jon said as the phone rang a second time. After the phone rang for the fourth time, Jon rose from his bed and looked around the room. "Man, when did he leave?" Jon asked himself aloud as he climbed out of his bed and picked up the phone receiver.

"Hello! . . . "This is Jon Quest, who is this?" . . . "From where?" . . . "You wanna do a story about what?" . . . "Are you serious?" . . ."When?" . . ."How did you hear about this?" . . ."Yeah, right. Whatever. Fine." . . ."Tomorrow?" . . ."Yeah, tomorrow is fine. About 4:30?" . . ."Yeah, okay. Great. Meet us at the library, which is the first building on your right as you come through the main gate." . . ."Okay we'll see you then."

Jon hung up the phone and for a moment was still. Then he picked the phone back up and dialed Tim's number.

"Hello."

"Hey, Vince, whassup?"

"Oh, hey, Jon. Nuttin' much. How you doin'?"

"I'm cool. Where's your room dog?"

"Right here. Hold on."

A moment later, Tim's voice greeted Jon. "Hey, Jon, whassup?"

"You busy tomorrow afternoon?"

"What time?"

"'Bout 4:30."

"I gotta go to boxing practice, but I can be done by then. Why?"

"*Athletics Illustrated* just called and they want to do a story about the 'Tiger Towel.'"

"Yeah? Cool!"

"We're meeting them at the library."

"All right. You want me to come to your room or meet you over there?"

"Why don't you meet me in front of the barracks at 4:00."

"All right."

"Talk to you later."

"Peace."

Several weeks later, Jon sat in the stands at the Homecoming game and looked up into the crowd. There were 'Tiger Towels' everywhere. He looked at Tim and smiled. Tim's idea had certainly been a good one. They had done extremely well.

There had been an article in the *Ebony Chronicle*. There was also an article in the school newspaper, which even had a picture of Jon and Tim presenting two 'Tiger Towels' to General Helmsley. There was an article in *Athletics Illustrated* as well. And there was the story that ran on Channel 7. Then there was the table they had set up in the lobby of the student activity center. They had sold every towel they produced. They had 250 towels made and between selling in the barracks and the student activity center, they had none left. They didn't even have any left for themselves. But as Jon looked at the crowd and smiled, his eyes fell upon something which instantly erased that smile he wore from his face.

Several cadets were waving confederate flags. As they waved the flags, they looked at Jon and flipped him the bird. Jon stared at them for a long while with a poker face. He could feel the anger as it welled up inside him.

One dinosaur which will never be extinct is the dinosaur of igno-rance, prejudice and racism, Jon thought.

As for the Homecoming game that day, the M.U.T.S. beat a cross-state rival that the school had not beaten in over fifteen years.

CHAPTER 20

"**G**eez, I knew it was bad down in Dixie. But I did not know it was like that," sighed Marcus. "Man, that place was bad!"

"IS bad," corrected Joyell. "Nothing's changed. They have just found a different way to do it."

"Yeah, just like everywhere else in this country," insisted Angelo.

"So, they kept flyin' that flag, huh?" said Marcus.

"Yep," answered Jon, obviously a thousand miles away.

Lexie, sitting next to Jon on the love seat, reached out and caressed his arm. Jon smiled when he felt her soft touch.

"I think I'm gonna hurl!" said Joyell in her best "valley girl" voice.

"N-E-Way!" said Lexie, putting up her hand, palm side facing Joyell.

"So did the flags ever stop flyin'? I mean did you ever replace them completely?" asked Marcus.

"Nah. Not with all them ignorant rednecks down there," replied Bernice.

"She's right. The odds were definitely against us. But more than that, the odds were against me. At that point I was playing in a game where the dealers had a stacked deck. But I thank God He gave me the strength and wisdom so I could play their game, and eventually beat them at it!"

———————————

Jon sat in his room while doing homework from his constitutional law class. This was one of his favorite and most interesting classes. Jon loved law and politics. His love for business prompted him to declare his major to be international law and political intelligence. His love for business prompted him to declare business marketing as his minor. Amazingly enough, even with a double major and never having attended summer school, Jon was due to graduate in only four years. This, undoubtedly, was because Jon typically took 21 hours per semester, or more.

Not bad for a "nigger", he thought, smiling wryly to himself.

While Jon sat in his room, he was aware of the brisk cold air that swirled around the outside of his window. He was aware of the constant banging from the noisy radiator in his room. Even though it was noisy, the radiator always kept his room warm. Often, he would have to turn the radiator off to escape the sauna it would quickly create.

Jon, pausing from his homework, now looked out of his window. Darkness had covered the outside like a giant foreboding cloak. Yet, as Jon glanced through the bars, the darkness teased him. It reminded Jon who was inside, trapped behind bars, and who was outside roaming free. It reminded him of the essential nature of human freedom.

It reminded him that the only "black" thing that was truly free in America was indeed the night.

The phone rang and startled Jon. Jon looked at the phone as it rang again. Based on the ring, Jon knew that the call was coming from somewhere on campus. *Cool*, he thought.

"Quest here," he said in his typical military tone.

"Cadet Quest?"

"Yeah? Who's this?"

"This is Cadet Captain Crawford, Honor Committee Chairman."

Jon paused a moment. *Hmmm, what the fuck does he want?* wondered Jon.

"Yeah, so?" responded Jon.

"Cadet Quest, I need to come by at 10:30 and talk to you."

"About what?"

"Well, I need to talk to you in person."

"Not tonight you won't."

"Yes tonight," insisted the Cadet on the other end of the phone.

"Look, cuz," Jon said after letting out a loud, exaggerated sigh, "I got things to do tonight at 10:30. So if you need to talk to me, come see me after Muster tomorrow morning."

"This won't wait!"

"It will have to!"

"Don't piss me off, boy! I'm the only friend you got right now!"

"Yeah, well with friends like you, who the fuck needs enemies!" retorted Jon as he slammed the receiver down.

That is weird. I need to do some investigation. What in the world could the Honor Court want to talk to me about? What have they trumped up on one of my boyz? thought Jon. Jon's thoughts were interrupted when he heard a trumpet blowing, which signaled the end of study period.

Oh, shit! Is it 10:30 already? Jon quickly changed out of his daily uniform and into his running clothes. *Can't keep the little pledges waiting!* he thought as he rushed out of his room. As he headed out of the barracks, he could have sworn he heard someone calling his name. Behind his barracks, Jon met up with his fraternity brothers and several pledges that were all out for an "evening jog."

"Let's take them down to the marsh," suggested Neal.

"Great idea," agreed Kevin.

The group turned and headed over a small hill polluted with military workout equipment. They continued across a field, through the dimly lit night until they reached the edge of the marsh.

The pledges, clad in warm-up suits, stood at attention with their hoods pulled over their heads. Jon's fraternity brothers surrounded the pledges and began barking commands and questions in rapid-fire fashion. As this "evening jog" continued, Jon pulled one of his fraternity brothers to the side. "Tim, c'mere a sec," said Jon.

Tim walked over and removed his hood. "Yeah?" said Tim.

"I got a phone call tonight."

"Yeah? From who?"

"The chairman of the Honor Committee."

"Whaaaaaaat! Uh oh! It must be your time now. Let's see . . . they got Adam and Hal. You had to know they were coming for you!"

"Yeah, I guess so. But I still am curious to know how. Remember with Hal it was cheating. With Adam, they accused him of going AWOL and then lying about it. What will it be for me?"

"Hmmmm, who knows? When do they want to meet with you?"

"Now."

"Excuse me?"

"They wanted to meet tonight . . . at 10:30."

"Yeah, so why are you here?"

"I told them I was busy."

"Man, you got some big fuckin' balls!"

"Yeah, Zulu balls, babeee! But what difference does it make if I piss them off? They are obviously coming after me. So as far as I'm concerned, the gloves are off. No need for me to try to be

184

nice and accommodating while they are trying to kick my black ass outta here!"

"True dat! True dat!"

"So, what the fuck, if they gonna come aftah me, I'm gonna be ready and waitin' on 'em."

As the two walked back toward the others, Tim suddenly stopped and grabbed Jon by the arm. "Yo, if you need us . . .," said Tim.

"Yeah, Tim, I know. I know. Thanks, that means a lot to me," said Jon.

There was a knock at Jon's door.

"C'min," called Jon.

Jon's door opened and two White cadets walked through. They looked around the room as if surveying it.

"What can I do for you?" Jon said dryly.

"Cadet Quest?"

"As if you didn't know."

"I'm Cadet Captain Crawford and this is Cadet Captain Evans. Let me get straight to the point. We are here to advise you that you have been brought up on the Honor Court violation of stealing."

Jon, who was leaning back in the chair at this desk, looked incredulously at the two.

"Stealing? Stealing what?" he said calmly.

"Stealing a phone calling card," answered the second cadet.

"A calling card? Yeah, right! Whose?"

"Aaron Harris'."

"My roommate? You've got to be kidding!"

"On the contrary," snarled the second cadet, "we are quite serious, Cadet Quest. We need to advise you of the severity of this charge and your corresponding rights."

"My rights? Fuck that! Let me tell you about your rights!" Jon said, rising from his desk. "You have the right to get the hell out of my room with that bullshit! How am I gonna steal my own roommate's calling card?"

"Well, according to him—"

"He's buggin'!"

"Well, he said you have been using his card without his authorization."

"Bullshit."

"He said there are over one hundred dollars' worth of calls which can be traced directly to you."

"Well, I'll talk to him and see . . ."

"You are forbidden to talk to him regarding this matter."

Jon thought for a moment. He hadn't really talked to Aaron lately. He always left early and came back late. When he was in the room, he was unusually silent and had been acting very strange lately. But Jon hadn't paid any of it much attention. If Aaron never spoke, that actually would not have bothered Jon.

"So, this is it. This is how y'all are gonna try to do it?" he said.

"Excuse me?" came the seemingly bewildered response.

"There are no excuses, mutha fucka! You go back and tell whoever sent you that they are gonna have to come stronger than this. This is beneath them. I woulda thought they had more imagination. More creativity. But this? Puhleez!" exclaimed Jon.

"What are you talking about?" retorted the cadets.

"Nothing. Fuck it! So, what now?" asked Jon.

Well, we need to know how you are gonna plead, then we'll know what to do next," responded the Captain Evans.

"Innocent, of course," Jon snorted.

"Well, then I guess there will be a trial. We have to report this to the Committee, and we will get back with you. We will be back tomorrow night at 10:30. Be here!"

"Yeah, whatever."

"Good luck, Cadet Quest," said Cadet Crawford with a contemptuous grin.

The cadets looked at one another with devious grins, rose and exited the room.

Jon, saw the look they gave one another and knew this situation was worse than he thought.

He picked up the phone and dialed the familiar number. The phone rang two times before someone on the other end answered.

"Yeah?"

"Whazzup, Nig?"

"You, dog."

"I need to talk to you this afternoon. I need you to erase a little story for me."

"No prob. When and where?"

"The park off the yard at 4:06."

"Cool."

Later that night, Jon lay on his bed feeling the familiar fatigue he had known all year. The fatigue created by Jon's never really sleeping at night. The fatigue created by Jon's always being on guard. The fatigue created by Jon's always trying to stay a step ahead. As he lay there fighting this familiar and unwelcome friend and listening to Aaron's rhythmic breathing, he remembered the warning he had given to Aaron in the beginning of the year when Aaron had approached him asking if they could room together.

"Yeah, Aaron, that's cool. However, do not ever cross me. Do not ever try to sell me down the river. Do not repeat what you hear or see in this room. If you ever do, I guarantee this campus will not be large enough for you to hide on," Jon had said.

As Jon lay in the darkness, he suddenly became aware of others in his room. He heard movement and breathing. He then heard a flutter of fabric. Suddenly, there was more movement, muffled yells, and whispering coming from the rack across the room. The whispering voices continued.

"You were warned, you stupid mutha fucka!"

"You don't know who you crossed, do you White boy?"

"You didn't have a calling card stolen!"

"You loaned the card to your roommate once or twice!"

"You were mistaken about the calls. Later when you looked again, you remembered you had made the calls."

"You fucked with the wrong niggah, boy!"

"Be careful, for you never know what lurks in the night."

"You never know what may strike or where it may strike."

"You don't want to fuck with us! Nobody in their right mind wants to fuck with us."

"We move like the darkness and nothing chases us before we have struck!"

"If you don't remember that you did give authorization and that those calls belong to you, then just like the night, we will return at the end of each day. It won't matter where you go, we'll find you. No matter what you do, you can't stop the onslaught of the night!"

As Jon listened, he detected muffled screaming and crying. Then, as quickly and quietly as they had come, the whispering voices were gone. All that was left was quiet sobs and groans.

Jon turned toward the wall. Now he could give in to his familiar friend. Now Jon could sleep.

The next day, the charges were dropped.

CHAPTER 21

"**W**ow! You have got to be kidding me!" exclaimed Marcus.
Jon sat at the table, all eyes on him as the painful memories washed over him. He was motionless and barely coherent. It was as if the memories had paralyzed him and prodded him, all at the same time.

This feeling had continued throughout Jon's life. He had never released any of this out of his mind. Jon had pushed past these feelings, but little things here and there would always bring him back there. Little things could bring the memories crashing back, like large waves upon the wet sand. Just like the waves of the sea, Jon often felt that every wave that washed over him took a little more sand away, each time.

Jon felt like he was eroding, much like those beaches Lexie so loved visiting. With every wave, more and more grains of his sand floated away. It had been all Jon could do to not allow what happened to him at M.U.T.S. define his life.

In fact, for many years after he had graduated, which had been a fiasco in and of itself, Jon had refused to wear the ring from M.U.T.S. Jon had kept the ring in a wooden box housed in his top chest drawer. He did not open it. He did not look at it. It did not exist in his alternate reality.

But it did exist.

It existed in ways that made Jon better. It existed in ways that would, later in life, remind Jon he could persevere. It existed in ways that showed Jon that no matter how large the wave, he could ride it.

In fact, a few years after Jon had graduated, Jon Sr. had visited him and noticed that Jon was not wearing his ring.

"Where is your ring?" inquired Jon Sr.

"In my drawer."

"Why isn't it on your finger?"

"Dad, I don't ever want to wear that ring! I don't want anyone knowing I graduated from there," remarked Jon, anger welling up in his chest.

"Really? So, all that you went through and all that you endured, you are just going to tuck that away quietly so people can't see your strength? With all you went through, you should never take it off! It is a sign of victory and perseverance. It is a sign of how you overcame all that they threw at you. Wearing your ring is not about them, it is about you! Do what you want to do, but, given how much that ring cost, and I don't mean in dollars and cents, you should wear it proudly and never take it off!"

Jon was stunned. He never thought of those things his father mentioned. The first thing Jon realized was how amazing it was to hear Jon Sr. talk so much about his situation. Jon Sr. was a man of few words and rarely talked very long or said very much. His words were often few and far between but always laced with wisdom.

In those words that Jon Sr. just said to Jon, he had literally invested years of wisdom, which Jon would not ignore. From that day forward, Jon wore the ring on a regular basis.

"Jon, you really went through some crap! How in the world do you not hate that place?" remarked Angelo, interrupting Jon's thoughts and bringing him back to reality.

"Who says he doesn't?" interjected Bernice.

"Nah, I don't hate it. I have mental scars from M.U.T.S., but I don't hate it. It is hard for me to reconcile the pain with the benefits, but I don't hate it," said Jon quietly.

"Well, I know I would hate it," exclaimed Angelo. "Pass the banana pudding, please."

Jon smiled, nodded his head, and stood up. He looked around the table at his family, who were preoccupied with other things now.

Yeah, it is so easy for them to switch gears. It is easy for others to just move on. But for those of us who lived it . . . not so much, Jon thought.

The phone in Jon's room rang.

"Oh, my fuckin' god!" groaned Jon as he reached for the phone. "Hello?"

"Hey, JJ," said the bubbly voice on the other end of the phone. "You still gonna pick me up?"

"What? Huh? What are you talking about, Bernice? Pick you up from where?"

"Surprise!"

"What?"

"I said surprise, Niggah! I came to see you graduate!"

"No way!" exclaimed Jon, sitting up in his bed.

"Way!" sang Bernice. "But I was kidding about picking me up. Mom and Dad are picking me up. I just wanted to call you really early in the morning because I am sure you were out getting drunk or having sex or both last night. So, I figured I would call you extra early and see how your hangover is doing!"

"Oh, you got jokes?"

"Nah, just wanted my little brother to know that I love him so much, I rode for two days on a bus to see him walk across that stage! I am so glad you are leaving, Jon!"

"You and me both!"

"So, anyway I am waiting for Mom and Dad to get here. Then I'll go back to the hotel so I can shower cuz a sistah is funky!"

"Yes, please make sure you baptize yourself before coming out here!"

"Oh, trust me!"

"Bernice?"

"Yeah?"

"Thank you."

There was a pause.

"You're welcome, baby bruh."

Several hours later, Jon sat in the middle of a sea of gray. He shifted in his seat and waved away a fly. Jon hated flies. One of his biggest irritants was standing at attention on the Parade Deck as flies and mosquitoes had their way with him and the other cadets. Every Friday during parade, Jon was convinced there was a big sign posted for all the flies, gnats, and mosquitoes that read: "All You Can Eat Smorgasbord." During his freshman year, Jon had to stand there and serve as a meal for these vexatious insects. Now, as Jon sat outside in the typically muggy Southern air, he knew this was the last time.

The last time the insects would feast upon him.

The last time he would have to have his head on a swivel.

The last time he would see this place.

Jon promised himself that once he was done, he would never come back. *For what?* he would say to himself. *Why would I come back here? A place where I am hated and a place I hate?*

True to his word, since his graduation, Jon had not been back. He never planned on going back.

Jon was brought back from his thoughts as the cadet sitting next to him, nudged him.

"Time to go!" said the cadet.

All the cadets on Jon's row were standing and preparing to walk toward the stage to have their degrees conferred upon them. Years of hard work. Years of studying. Years of going without. Years of focusing on this day. Now, "one day" was here.

Jon walked stiffly toward the stage and moved into his place in the long gray line.

Jon did not know where his family was, but he was sure they were there. Jon Sr., Kathy, Bernice, Joyell, and Jon's grandfather.

Jon's grandfather, whose father was born a slave.

Wow, thought Jon. *I am only a couple of generations removed from America's original sin.*

Jon's mother's father's father was a slave and here Jon was graduating from a prestigious, southern military university. This southern military university that one generation ago did not permit African-Americans to attend. This southern military university that celebrated the "war of Northern aggression". This southern military university whose founders fought to keep Jon's ancestors in slavery.

Slavery, the violent abduction of a group of people, who were taken to a hostile land, stripped of their identity, robbed of their history, required to adopt foreign names, practices, and religions, forced to build the world's greatest economy on their free labor, while their women were regularly raped, their men were regularly castrated, their families were ripped apart, they were sold and treated like chattel, and their lives did not matter. Slavery, a heinous institution so important to the wealth, prosperity, and well-being of a group of states and statesmen that they were willing to wage a bloody, protracted war to protect its future and their stolen existence. Slavery, the psychological domination of a people, the physical abuse of people, and the historical trivialization of its effects on future generations. Slavery, a practice so savage and brutal, that hundreds of years later it haunts the minds and lives of the descendants of those who through faith, capitulation, and submission, learned to survive. Slavery, an institution that has and continues to affect and infect an unrepentant nation.

Yet, here was the son of one of those slaves, a free man, watching his grandson graduate from a prestigious institution that trained young men to fight for the continued existence of . . . slavery. The irony was striking.

"ROBERT WILLIAM QUARRELL," called the voice.

Jon snapped back to reality. He was next. As Jon positioned himself next to the bottom stair of the stage, he looked out over the audience. There were hundreds of people there. Jon saw a sea of White faces. Some chubby. Some slender. Some pale. Some blushed. Some tanned.

As Jon looked out among the crowd, he could not help but think to himself, *what do they have against diversity? Against being different? No two people are alike, so why do they hate my black skin so much?*

"JONATHAN HEZEKIAH QUEST," called the voice.

As Jon walked up the stairs, there was one unmistakable sound. Hissing. In the Corps of Cadets, there was a way to show patent disapproval or dislike of something, or someone, and it was to hiss. And from the time Jon's name was announced, that was the only sound you could hear on the parade deck, on that muggy southern morning. The sound rang out loudly. It was deafening.

Jon was handed his college degree and he turned toward the crowd. For a moment, Jon stood looking across the faces twisted with hate. He looked at the men who would be officers in the U.S. Armed Forces. Some of those who were hissing would become colonels and generals. Some would lead men and women into war. Some would fly high above wars and drop bombs. Some would order the loved ones of others into combat. Some would become politicians—mayors, congressmen, senators, governors.

Some would become CEOs of companies with all races working for them. But, here they were, eyes and faces full of hatred and vitriol. Here they were bonded together by hatred. Hatred of someone who dared to break the silence. Hatred of someone who would not shuffle and fetch. Hatred of someone who "did not know his place." Hatred of someone who fought against racism and ignorance. Hatred of someone who dared to think his life and the lives of others like him mattered. Yes, these were the leaders of tomorrow, infected with the hatred of yesterday.

Suddenly, Jon heard cheering and yelling. He squinted and looked to see from where the yelling and ruckus was coming. As he looked out, he heard someone yell his name.

Toward the back of the parade deck he saw people moving and being pushed aside. The entire ceremony paused as the ruckus grew louder. And then Jon saw Bernice and Joyell. They were walking proudly down the center of the parade deck, moving people, yelling his name, shaking pom-pom sticks, and cheering. As they yelled and cheered, they took time to stare down anyone foolish enough to stare, not move, or say something to them.

At that moment, Jon swelled with pride. At that moment he was convinced Bernice rode on a bus for two days to get to his graduation to do exactly what she was doing and hope someone would say something, anything, crazy to her.

Jon turned and walked toward the edge of the stage as the ceremony continued. As Jon neared the edge of the stage, a uniformed African-American police officer stepped forward to greet him.

"Mr. Quest, we are going to escort you out of here."

The police officer placed his hand on Jon's right bicep.

"Follow me, Sir," he said, smiling.

Jon followed the policeman down the steps. As he walked, several other people in various uniforms followed closely behind them. There were also two men in suits, following the contingent. Jon recognized one of them as the FBI agent assigned to him early in his senior year. He caught Jon's eye and smiled. As they ushered Jon out toward a side door and into a navy-blue Ford Crown Victoria with darkly tinted windows, Jon smiled and finally, he exhaled. Finally, after four years. Finally, after countless physical attacks. Finally, after changed grades. Finally, after severed relationships. Finally, after being called nigger as if it appeared on his birth certificate. Finally, after having food withheld. Finally, after being shot at. Finally, after almost being run down. Finally, after his closest friends were all summarily and surgically removed from the university, after which several of them would meet an early death. Finally, after fighting for what was pledged on paper but never in hearts. Finally. He. Exhaled.

Jon's entire family followed behind the Crown Victoria as it drove to the outskirts of town. Once there, they pulled over.

"Sir, we are going to follow you to the state line," said one of the policemen, whom Jon noticed had a patch that read "State Police."

Jon got out of their car and walked over to the van where his parents and grandfather sat. Bernice was driving Jon's car, which was parked immediately behind the van, with Joyell in the passenger seat. Joyell scampered into the small back seat as Bernice got out of the car, walked around to the passenger side, and got in.

Jon looked over his shoulder toward the town where he had lived the past four years. He paused a moment, then climbed into the driver's seat of his car, started it up, shifted into first, sped away, and did not look back.

CHAPTER 22

J on sat on the screened-in deck of his home in his favorite chair. The chair was a wrought iron rocker, with a plush cushion. Positioned in front of the chair was a matching ottoman, with a matching cushion. Next to the chair was a small wine refrigerator, stocked with Gewürztraminer, Sauternes, Beaujolais, Malbec, and Montepulciano. On top of the wine chiller sat an aroma candle, an iPod player, and an ashtray for his cigars.

Outside of his bedroom, this room was Jon's favorite. The deck room was the best of both worlds. He was outside, which allowed him to enjoy the beautiful setting as the wind rustled through the trees. He was able to see the beautiful sunset, take in the beautiful blues skies, and hear the crashing of the waves on the nearby rocks. He was able to sit there during a rainstorm and be a part of nature. Conversely, he was not tormented by the fury of bugs flying around the screens, determined to find a way inside. He did not have to worry about swatting and spraying. He was "in the outside," but not "of the outside."

The screened-in deck was tastefully decorated. On one end were two matching wrought iron rockers, with ottomans. On another side was an outside dining set, with two highchairs and a high table. The table had a multicolored marble center, on which sat a stack of granite coasters with a "Q" monogram. On the other side of the room was a hammock for two. The metal on the hammock matched the wrought iron rockers and the dining table. The hammock itself was a multicolored dream coat design, with honey brown rope fixtures. Finally, on the final side of the room was the pièce de résistance—the hot tub!

The room was truly a retreat and one which Jon retired to every evening after the meal. It was his place of solitude and peace. It was his place to regroup and exhale. In this room of respite, Jon could become lost in his thoughts and enjoy the reflection and introspection that brought so much inner healing and growth. Jon would often sit with a cigar and a glass of wine, listening to his favorite "Quiet Storm" playlist for hours.

"Mind if I join you?"

Jon turned toward the door and smiled as his "Beautiful Angel" stood, extending a glass of Montepulciano.

"Even if you were not bearing gifts, I would not mind!"

"Good."

Lexie took her rightful place—in her chair, next to Jon, and for several moments was silent.

"I know recounting all of that is difficult for you," said Lexie quietly.

"Yeah, some of those wounds have not quite healed," agreed Jon. "When they heal, they leave scars, and from time to time when you touch the scars, there is still discomfort."

Lexie nodded in agreement.

After another pause, she added, "But as I always say, Jon. Your scars are not for you, even when they hurt. They are for others to know they can make it through whatever they are going through, and still live."

"Hmmm," grunted Jon. Again, he was a million miles away, lost in his own thoughts. "But am I living? Am I truly living? What so many people do not understand is that the mental pain lasts far longer than the physical discomfort. For a person subjected to abuse, just stopping the abuse doesn't stop the pain and mental anguish."

Jon reflected on the impact his years at M.U.T.S. had on him. He thought about the ulcers it had caused, even as a young man. He thought about the paranoia. He thought about the mistrust of other cultures and ethnicities. He wondered how much it added to his life . . . and how much it took away.

Jon had recently spoken to a number of alumni that attended M.U.T.S. and someone posed a question. The question was, "If you had it to do all over again, would you attend M.U.T.S., would you have attended an HBCU or would you have gone elsewhere?"

Jon had to seriously examine that question.

Of course, his immediate and obvious answer was:

Hell, no! I would have never come to this hell hole!

However, Jon seriously pondered the question, examining it from all sides.

Lexie was an HBCU graduate. She was so proud of her HBCU, always bragging about her education, her enlightenment, her opportunities, the validation that shaped the confident African-American woman she was. She extolled the virtues of receiving an education at a place that wanted you to succeed versus a place that hated you and the very fact that you were there. In her mind, how could there even be a remote comparison?

As Jon thought about this, he reached out and picked up his glass of wine.

Jon rolled the dark red beverage around in the large bowl, watching the legs form. He put it up to his mouth, and as he turned the glass up slightly, he noticed the glimmer on his hand.

His ring. His M.U.T.S. ring.

Jon's university ring was large and made out of pure gold. No gaudy stones. No hollow shank. Pure gold, through and through. Jon thought for a moment, staring at his ring.

This ring had to go through fire. This ring had to go through the flames. If it did not go through the fire and the flames, it would not have been pure enough for its designation of 14-karat pure gold.

Jon imagined when the jeweler first started working with that very piece of metal.

It was likely dull and imperfect. It was likely lumpy and unattractive. It had no distinguishing marks. It likely would not have fetched $1 at a yard sale. But look at it now. Look at it now. Beautiful. Shiny. Bearing etchings of meaning all over. Heavy. Expensive. Now that it had gone through the fire and the flames, that $1 lump of metal was worth hundreds. Thousands!

As Jon reflected on his ring, he found his answer.

Yes. Yes, I would have attended M.U.T.S. I would have exposed myself to the fire. I would not have complained about the flames. M.U.T.S. made me the man I am. It gave me these scars (etchings) and each scar tells a story of survival and strength. Each scar, inflicted with military precision, is evidence of tenacity, perseverance, wisdom, and strength. It is because of M.U.T.S. that I entered a $1 boy and exited a million-dollar man! It is because of M.U.T.S. that I became the man, the father, the husband, the executive that I am. God had a purpose for me, and who is to say that purpose did not go through M.U.T.S.? None of us know God's plan for us or the journey that gets us to that plan. All we can do is allow God to order our steps and trust in Him. M.U.T.S. did not kill me. M.U.T.S. made me stronger.

Jon briefly paused, stood up and walked to the edge of his screened in deck. Looking at God's beautiful nature, he thought,

While the experience was unpleasant at times, it created the scars that have given others hope. Come to think of it, if I would not have stayed or never would have attended M.U.T.S., who's to say that the Black alumnus that posed the question would have even been there? Our vision is so small, so limited that all we can see is ourselves and our pain. We cannot see the impact our lives have on the people we cannot see, will not see, or will never know. How many people have made it because I am here? How many people have stood on my shoulders that I do not even know? How many people's shoulders am I standing on that I do not know?

Jon's eyebrow raised as he continued,

No, I will not be selfish and say I would not have gone to M.U.T.S. because I can never know how my going there and staying there has opened the door, or cleared the path, for those behind me that I will never know. While I was there, it hurt. While I was there, many people tried to run me out. What they did not know was that I had a purpose. What they did not know was that my life is bigger than me. What they did not know was that they thought they were fighting me, but they were really fighting God's purpose for me. Yes, they did me wrong. They set traps for me. They built gallows, rejoicing for the day when I would hang from them. Yes, they did evil by me. But what they meant for evil, God turned to good.

Jon smiled to himself.

I should have known from the beginning, just by the name, what I was getting myself into! I should have known M.U.T.S. was full of bad dogs! Oh, the irony!

ACKNOWLEDGMENTS

A heartfelt thank you to all the people who suffered so this book could be written. May sensitivity and empathy guide the hearts and minds of those who have never permanently been the minority in a majority world. While it may not have happened to you, it does not hurt any less to those to whom it did happen.

A special thanks to the people whose shoulders I stand on: strong men like Chip, Vince, and Carl who inspired me, challenged me, and guided me across the burning sands; Mr. Morris, who taught me how to change the rules to suit my strengths; Dr. Willette, who supported me, believed in me, and guided me through a land fraught with danger and was always my "base"; Dr. Elise, who challenged me, pushed me, supported me, and helped me be the man I needed to be; Mr. Pyatt, who was an inspiration, guide, and sage through my journey; Rev. Dr. Rivers, who brought the calvary to ensure justice was done and who ended up becoming a wonderful friend; Commissioner Mignon and Pastor Alfrieda, who helped me tell the truth of my story and to whom I gave exclusive access; Fredricka, who helped tell the truth of my story on television and to whom I gave exclusive access; and Pontheolla, who supported me, guided me, and helped me understand how to navigate shark filled waters.

A special thanks to my brother Jeff Meyer, who encouraged me to tell my truth through fiction and believed my story was a story worth telling. Tracey Baker-Simmons who encouraged me to finish my story and share it with the world.

Thank you to my family, who know, more so than anyone else, the difficulties of which this book speaks. Thank you to the countless people who gave me their ear as I tried to work through the pain and achieve catharsis.

A special thank-you to my editor and publisher for helping me to bring to life a story deeply embedded within me and tell it in a meaningful way.

A special thanks to those who put up with me, tolerated me, and gave me grace as the scars of my past presented themselves in my present.

And my most special thanks to my wonderful wife and beautiful angel, who encouraged me, believed in me, and gave me the space to recall my past as I sought to tell this story in real time. Thank you for allowing the early mornings and late nights; for comforting me while I relived some of the most difficult times in my life; for praying for me as I sought to do God's will for our lives; and for always allowing God's light to shine through you, as sometimes it was the only light I could see.

Thank-you to all who purchased this book and took a painful journey with me that ended in triumph.

Finally, thank-you to my God, who is big enough to be all our God, and who has made it so that what the enemy meant for evil, He turned to good.

ABOUT THE AUTHOR

Ken Gordon has been engaged in fighting for racial justice and serving the community since his high school days in New Jersey. He is a member of Alpha Phi Alpha fraternity, a Diamond Life Member of the NAACP, and the former president of an NAACP branch in New Jersey. He has served as deputy mayor of a small town in NJ, and is a former president of that town's board of education, as well as having been the Chair of Human Relations Commissions in Colorado and New Jersey.

Ken is a highly sought-after speaker on leadership, public service, civil rights, HIV/AIDS education, political action, and youth mentoring, and is the former host of a weekly one-hour radio show and a weekly one-hour cable television show aimed at finding solutions to common community issues.

He is married with four children and lives in Alabama.

CPSIA information can be obtained
at www.ICGtesting.com
Printed in the USA
BVHW041830240321
603359BV00017B/579